DID YOU ENJOY THE KISS?" REID DEMANDED.

Very much. Too much. "Don't be silly!" Polly replied. "I consider it merely research for my book."

He scowled. "Is that what you're still telling yourself?"

"Naturally. What else could it be?"

"Beats me." Then he grinned wickedly. "But I believe in research." Slowly and boldly, his gaze slid over her body before capturing her eyes with a sizzling look. "So let's see if practice makes perfect," he drawled, then kicked the door shut and stunned her with a kiss that was hotter, wetter, even more sensual than last time. . . .

WHAT ARE *LOVESWEPT* ROMANCES?

They are stories of true romance and touching emotion. We believe those two very important ingredients are constants in our highly sensual and very believable stories in the LOVESWEPT *line. Our goal is to give you, the reader, stories of consistently high quality that may sometimes make you laugh, sometimes make you cry, but are always fresh and creative and contain many delightful surprises within their pages.*

Most romance fans read an enormous number of books. Those they truly love, they keep. Others may be traded with friends and soon forgotten. We hope that each LOVESWEPT *romance will be a treasure—a "keeper." We will always try to publish*

LOVE STORIES YOU'LL NEVER FORGET
BY AUTHORS YOU'LL ALWAYS REMEMBER

The Editors

BAD
ATTITUDE

DORIS
PARMETT

BANTAM BOOKS
NEW YORK · TORONTO · LONDON · SYDNEY · AUCKLAND

BAD ATTITUDE

A Bantam Book / November 1993

If you would be interested in receiving protective vinyl covers for your
Loveswept books, please write to this address for information:

Loveswept
Bantam Books
P.O. Box 985
Hicksville, NY 11802

ISBN 0-553-44251-1

Published simultaneously in the United States and Canada

Bantam Books are published by Bantam Books, a division of Bantam Doubleday Dell Publishing Group, Inc. Its trademark, consisting of the words
"Bantam Books" and the portrayal of a rooster, is Registered in U.S. Patent
and Trademark Office and in other countries. Marca Registrada. Bantam
Books, 1540 Broadway, New York, New York 10036.

PRINTED IN THE UNITED STATES OF AMERICA

OPM   0 9 8 7 6 5 4 3 2 1

For my California friend,
Phyllis Newman. I'll never think of
green without remembering your phone call.
Thanks.

ONE

Polly Sweet listened in growing disbelief to the tall, lean, dark-haired Pennsylvania state policeman who stood before the fireplace in the den she'd converted into her office. Detective Reid Cameron had interrupted her at the worst possible moment, while she was writing a tender love scene, a scene she'd struggled with for most of the day. If she didn't stick to her schedule, she couldn't possibly finish the romance novel before school started in the fall. After spending nine months with energetic kindergartners, she'd eagerly looked forward to her summer hiatus.

She would not allow him to ruin her plans with his preposterous scheme.

"No," she said when he finished his explanation. "It's out of the question. I will not allow you to use my house for your command post."

"Ms. Sweet," he said, lowering his voice in contrast

to the way she'd raised hers. "You've got the terminology wrong. Your house isn't being used for anything."

"Not according to what you told me."

"I'm obligated to protect you."

She frowned at the thoroughness of his steady gaze, which moved over her as if she were under a microscope. She'd dressed for comfort that morning in a pair of frayed white cutoffs and an old, snug sleeveless cotton top.

"That's a matter of opinion," she retorted, planting her hands at her waist to signal her irritation. "If I say I don't need your protection, I don't. If I say I live a quiet life in the country, take my word for it. Surely you can see I'm far from wealthy. The few pieces of jewelry I own are fake, nothing to tempt a jewel thief. Do you really expect me to buy your absurd story?"

"I expect you to listen to reason," he said as she paced in front of the window.

She turned toward him, scowling. "No jewel thief with an ounce of brains would stash a cache of diamonds here. Why would he choose this place? It isn't easily accessible. You know that, you had to cross my private bridge to get here. I suggest you return to your headquarters and check your facts. If it makes you feel better, you may inform your superiors you've fulfilled your duty by telling me. Thank you and good day."

She marched past him through the homey room, filled with family mementos and the comfortable furniture her parents had loved. Out in the hall she flung open the front door. While she didn't want to appear rude, she couldn't allow herself to get bogged down in conversation. Not with the crucial love scene waiting. When she felt the warm June breeze caress her face and she didn't hear footsteps at her back, she spun around. Nothing. She'd shown herself the door! Marching back into the den, she found Reid Cameron leaning forward, knees slightly bent, peering at a mural her father had painted.

"Detective Cameron, I thought I made myself clear. In case I didn't, I'll repeat myself. My intention when I awoke this glorious morning was to spend the whole day writing, stop around six, prepare dinner, then relax with a cup of chamomile tea while I listen to the evening news. Following that, I would return here to my den, sit at this computer, and edit my day's efforts. This still remains my Thursday goal."

He peered over his shoulder at her and nodded. "Admirable. This is a terrific oil painting. Who did it?"

A special man, she thought. One she'd loved dearly and would always miss. A tall, strong man. A caring man who always found time for his inquisitive daughter. She'd loved watching him dab oils on his sable brush, then lift his hand to bring his vision of their land to life on the canvas.

"My father," she replied, a wistful note creeping into her voice.

Detective Cameron turned around, regarding her thoughtfully. "He's good. He shows an interesting combination of powerful strokes mixed with a lyrical touch."

It surprised her that this stranger found the same beauty in her father's painting as she did. "Yes, he did."

"Did?"

She felt the lump in her throat that always came when she thought of the loss of her father and, shortly afterward, her mother. The two people closest to her had died too young from injuries sustained in an automobile accident.

Blinking back her tears, Polly found herself gazing into a pair of sympathetic dark eyes. "My parents passed away several years ago. My father was a farmer who loved to paint."

"I'm sorry for your loss. I still miss my own dad. Do you set different goals for each day of the week, Ms. Sweet?"

"I'm sorry for your loss, too, Detective Cameron, but surely you have better things to do with your time than discuss my father's artistic abilities or my weekly calendar. It's three o'clock. Three precious hours left for me to accomplish my first draft."

"Your clock's fast. It's ten of three. Three hours and ten precious minutes, to be exact."

Polly caught his faint smile and decided she'd wasted enough time. By habit and nature, she meticulously planned her days. She never forgot a friend's or a relative's birthday. When her school principal asked for lesson plans, she delivered her book promptly. It suited her professional persona; it suited her disposition. Now her brain signaled a warning that unless she quickly got rid of this policeman, he would discover other interesting things in the room to waste her precious time.

"Thank you," she said. "I'll reset my watch after you leave. Again, good day."

A shadow of amused forbearance crossed his face. Without further comment or permission he sat down on a blue upholstered armchair, then indicated she should sit too.

"I hate putting a damper on your afternoon," he said, "but I'm afraid it doesn't work your way. You can't tell me what to do. I tell you what to do. Now please, sit down."

For a moment she debated getting the baseball bat she kept in the front closet and threatening him with it, but then she'd give him cause to arrest her. Her stomach clenched. She sat down.

He wasn't in uniform, and he didn't look like her idea of a cop. Though maybe on second thought, his rugged face, straight dark brows, and flashing white teeth did. His clothes didn't. He wore a denim jacket over jeans that clung to muscular thighs, and scruffy sneakers green with grass stains.

He leaned forward. "The man we're after, Aaron Grayson, isn't the brains behind the outfit that stole the jewelry. He's one player in what we know is a nationwide ring. The reasons you've given me against his coming here are exactly the reasons why he would use this place.

It's a perfect location to hide jewels, away from prying eyes. Also, he knows this section of western Pennsylvania like the back of his hand. He lived in the neighboring county until after he left high school. And may I remind you that you live alone."

"So what? A lot of women live alone. Right now I wish I *were* alone."

"Yes, many women live alone, but wouldn't you agree that most women don't live in an isolated location?"

"Don't play the statistics game with me, Detective."

"Ms. Sweet, we know Grayson could have come here without fear of being seen. We're fairly certain he hid the jewels here. Therefore, he'll return for them. Our information is, he will probably head back this way sometime over the next few days. You need me, Ms. Sweet."

She regarded him steadily. He didn't so much as blink. "No, I don't. I prefer to take my chances."

A slight smile lifted the corners of his mouth, the kind of sensual mouth she'd ascribed to the hero in her romance novel. Except her hero was malleable, reasonable. Gallant.

"The choice isn't yours," he said. "Grayson is dangerous. Until he's apprehended, I'm not leaving your side, Ms. Sweet. Day or night."

"What!" She sprang out of her seat. All his talk about missing jewels sounded like a bad movie script.

But his saying he wasn't leaving her side—day or night!—*that* sounded like real life. She couldn't allow it.

"I told you I live alone. It's the way I intend to live until I choose otherwise. My summers are precious to me. All year long I plan how I'll use my time. Use it, not squander it, to accomplish certain tasks I set for myself. My barn needs repairs. Barring my winning the lottery, which isn't likely, I'm obliged to work. That work requires privacy, solitude. As far as I'm concerned, you may set up all the roadblocks you want, as long as you set them on county property, which is on the other side of my bridge."

"No."

"Yes. I am far too busy to have you camped underfoot on the wild chance there are diamonds on my property. For example, Mr. Soames, a roofer, is coming to fix my barn tomorrow before it caves in. He kindly moved me up in his schedule after seeing how badly the roof needs repair. I'm sure you've noticed how saturated the ground is from our recent heavy rains. More rain is coming, either tomorrow or Saturday."

"Ms. Sweet, I suggest you call Mr. Soames and tell him not to come until next week. If you don't, I will. It's best coming from you. You can say you're leaving town unexpectedly."

His cool arrogance shocked her. "How dare you, Detective Cameron! Not only don't I want to cancel the roofer, you're asking me to tell a lie."

He didn't raise his voice, but calmly said, "That's right. Lie convincingly, but lie."

She shook her head, tossing her unruly blond hair. "Shame on you. And you call yourself a policeman. Some example you set."

"Your faith in police as role models is touching. Call it a cover story. Call it whatever you please. I'm not here to set an example. I'd appreciate the least amount of hassle possible." He paused, then added, "I have a court order to tap your phone."

She leaped out of her chair. "Whaaat?"

He ignored her outcry. "We have Grayson's voice print. If he calls pretending he's someone else, we'll know it's him. The fewer strangers on the property until he's captured, the better. I'm sorry to mess up your plans, but it can't be helped."

She stared at him, her gaze locked with his. There was an exasperating smile on his face, as if he knew, as a state policeman, he was acting within his rights. That by stating his duty was to protect her, he made his wishes supercede hers. He meant what he said. It wasn't fair. A wave of dizziness washed over her.

In seconds strong hands steadied her. Instinctively she grabbed them, holding on to them, feeling their strength. She experienced a nearly overwhelming desire to stay put and an equally strong desire, stemming from self-preservation, to move away. Aware that the uncommon tingling she felt came from the very person she hoped to get rid of, she disengaged her hands with a snap, flinging her palms up, indicating he was the last person she wanted touching her.

He had the decency to step back from her. "Ms. Sweet, I thought it best to get the bad news out of the way first."

"Did you? What's the good news?"

A grin tugged at his lips. "I'll be gone in a few days."

"If you think *that* makes me grateful, you're wrong. If you want to see grateful, leave. You barged into my home—"

"I rang the bell."

"Don't be cute. I asked you politely to leave. You refused. You order me around while telling me I should be afraid of a phantom thief. You're tapping my phone without my permission. How can you think that hiding behind the law as you insist on wrecking my privacy will make me feel better?"

"I assure you, whatever actions I take are for your protection."

She couldn't speak, she was that flabbergasted. Not for a minute did she feel her life in danger, unless it was from him. He was stealing her precious freedom. She eyed her computer screen longingly.

That morning she had awakened with such enthusiasm, joyous to see the sun streaming through her window. She'd welcomed a bright blue sky after five days of pounding rain, and had hurried to the barn to milk Horace, a cow incongruously named by Polly's elderly aunt Martha who lived across the road. The cow had been happy to leave the barn's confines after days of being cooped up. Polly's animal was happy; she was happy. Or she had been, until Reid Cameron's unwelcome arrival.

She studied his rough-hewn features. Damn him for resembling the hero in her book! Over lunch at school one day last month, she had led the conversation onto the kind of man her teacher friends liked to see as heroes. She knew they read romances. They didn't know she was writing one.

Her best friend, Grace Waters, had said, "Give me a gloomy, complex rebel, put us alone in a room with a single bed, then leave the rest to me."

Joan Daniels, the other kindergarten teacher, said, "Me too. I'll forget grading papers, shopping, taking my kids to the dentist, reminding them to practice piano. I'll forget about bills, carpooling, the works."

Lonni Landis wanted a hero whose burning dark gaze turned smoky with desire. She preferred him formidable, with a great body, yet manly enough to wear an earring. A sexy man, one who carried an aura of danger.

Grace summed it up for the three women. "We wouldn't change our husbands. We're not confusing reality with fantasy. It's harmless to escape for a few hours. What woman doesn't dream of a Rhett Butler striding into her life?"

Polly blinked. Her friends should meet Reid

Cameron. His profession met their condition for an element of danger. He was tall and had the requisite midnight-black hair and dark eyes. His broad shoulders tapered to a narrow waist. And he certainly looked formidable, standing before her with his arms folded in front of him, appearing about as movable as a granite statue. Give her a man with blond or light brown hair and blue or hazel eyes. Most important, he must possess a poetic soul, a man like Ashley Wilkes in *Gone With the Wind*.

Ashley was the essence of politeness. Ashley would never treat a lady rudely. She lifted her chin.

"I don't like you, Detective Cameron. I don't want you here. I disapprove of a man who forces his way into my private life, taps my phone, orders me to cancel my roofer, all under the guise of protecting me. So, no, I won't allow you to disrupt my life. Why can't you search the farm, find the jewels, and leave me alone?"

"We're after the whole gang, if possible. The people Grayson is associated with also deal drugs."

"All the more reason to leave me alone," she argued. "Catch him somewhere else."

He shook his head. "This is the best lead we've had in the two years we've been after this gang." He glanced at his watch. "My partner, Fran Mohr, will be here by dinnertime. Before then I'd like to check out the house and grounds."

How could her life get so complicated so quickly?

A teacher's salary didn't go far, and any extra money she had went into the care and upkeep of the house and property she'd inherited from her parents. Her love life was flat. She dated, but there was no one special. Her last serious romance had fizzled out three years ago. Was it any wonder she dreamed of selling her novel, of finally getting a break, of opening new doors?

"Detective Cameron, if you and your partner stay in my house, you'll abide by my rules. Otherwise you sleep outside."

As if he hadn't heard her, he strolled over to her desk and peered at the computer screen.

She grabbed his arm, blocking his view of the monitor. "That's the first rule! Stay away from my computer."

His unexpected smile was startling. It took her aback. The horrid man looked . . . handsome.

"So you write romances," he said. "My partner is hooked on them. I've never figured out their appeal."

"Figures. If you're trying to make points with me, you're losing. My second rule is that you never— *ever*—go near my bedroom."

His smile twisted. "When you see me in your bedroom, Ms. Sweet, I assure you it will be on official business."

He walked over to look at a little painting, a tranquil pastoral, that rested on an easel beside an occasional table.

"Your father's too?"

"Yes."

"Talented man." He turned to face her. "Ms. Sweet, just so you and I avoid trouble, let's clear up a few things. I am not your enemy. I know what I've told you hit you like a bolt from the blue."

"That's putting it mildly. It's unreal."

"You're wrong. It's real. Otherwise I'd never invade your privacy. If it helps, I didn't ask for this assignment. No one hopes more than I that we wrap up the case soon. Then"—he grinned—"you can get back to writing your sizzling romance."

"I think you're insufferable."

His smile broadened. "Good. We're off to an auspicious start."

Polly rolled her eyes.

"You and Fran will share your bedroom," he went on. "I don't want you left alone. The last time one of our people let a woman he was supposed to be guarding coerce him into leaving her side, an unfortunate accident happened to another trooper."

"What was it?"

"He stopped a bullet meant for her. Had she been where she belonged, he wouldn't have been shot."

Polly felt the blood drain from her face. Bullets killed. The man could have died. She stood silently for a few moments, her lips compressed.

"I'm stuck with you, aren't I?" she said finally.

"Yes." He spoke with as much reluctance as she.

"But think, when we return the diamonds to the insurance company, you'll collect a handsome reward."

"However much the check, it won't be enough!"

"Damn," he muttered as he started from the room. "I can see protecting you isn't going to be a bit of fun."

He went over her house like a bloodhound, not leaving a nook or cranny unexplored. He paced off halls, measuring them also for width. He ran up and down her staircase, testing which steps squeaked the most. He checked doors and windows for warping, checked the angles and views from each window. He prowled rooms, moving some furniture in order to have clear paths to the doors. He carried a twin bed from one of the spare rooms into her bedroom for his partner.

"Where is your partner?" Polly asked.

"Busy," he said shortly. Before setting up the bed, he removed his jacket to roll up his shirtsleeves. "She'll bring supplies with her when she comes later."

Polly's eyes widened when she saw the holster at his waist. Naturally he'd wear a gun. Cops wore a firearm. While she adjusted her mind to the unwelcome sight, he finished setting up the bed and said he'd take the room next door.

Polly bit back her smile. The mattress in the other bedroom was old and lumpy. And judging from his height of well over six feet, she guessed his feet would hang over the edge.

"There's one bathroom on this floor," she said,

walking back out into the hall. "I'll post a sched-ule."

He walked into the white tile bathroom. Several of her lacy bras hung on the shower rod, and she snatched them down.

"Are you assuming," he asked, "that nature calls on cue?"

Inhaling a deep breath, she counted to ten as he sauntered past her into the hall. "I meant if you want to use the shower. Keep up your fresh talk and you can swim in the river. The swift current should take you downstream fast. Providing you make it past the boulders."

He stopped and turned so swiftly, she was barely a few inches away from him. As she stared up into his dark eyes, she was disconcertingly aware of the heat emanating from his hard body.

"Ms. Sweet," he said in a near growl, "we'll get along fine if you stop trying to give me a hard time. For better or worse, you and I will be together for a while. If I swallowed my disappointment at having to do this, I suggest you do the same."

She glared up at him. "My third rule is you're never to try to intimidate me. I'll report you to your superiors."

He gave her a hard look. "For the record I like agreeable women. You are not agreeable. For the rec-ord my superiors sent me. For the record I can think of ten other places I'd rather be. Try to understand,

I'm not playing games." He turned to the stairs. "Now will you please show me where the cellar is?"

His insult galled her. She tromped down the stairs behind him, then stalked past him into the kitchen and jerked the cellar door open. "Since I'm forced to tolerate you, I'm going to write down a list of rules. I'll insist you follow them."

As if she hadn't spoken, he switched on the cellar light and started down the stairs, leaving her staring at his back.

Her heart sank. He'd made it clear that, for whatever reason, he resented being there as much as she wished he'd leave. Who knows? she thought, applying her writer's imagination. Maybe Detective Cameron and his partner, Fran Mohr, weren't getting along. Maybe they had mixed business with pleasure, and their romance had soured.

She peered out the window. The afternoon sunshine looked enticing. Marshmallow clouds dotted a blue sky. She'd planned on a long walk before dinner, but it looked as if that, too, had gone the way of her writing schedule.

With great reluctance she dialed Mr. Soames. His cheerful voice chilled after she offered Reid's excuse. Yes, he'd reschedule, but he couldn't say when. He'd reshuffled other customers as a special favor to her, he said, laying on the guilt. Then he added that the section of roof directly above the hayloft wasn't leaking. Yet.

She apologized profusely and quickly hung up.

Her hands were shaking. She looked at them in disgust. That was Reid Cameron's fault. He wasn't a figment of her fertile imagination. He was there all right, dark and domineering. What would her friends say if they knew?

Whether he liked it or not, while he was in her home, he'd abide by her guidelines. Taking pencil and paper, she sat down and started her list of rules. She set the times he could prepare his meals. She expected him to leave the kitchen spotless. Whatever he used, she expected him to replenish. If he dirtied the floors by walking around with muddy shoes, he'd be responsible for washing them. No towels on the bathroom floor. The bathroom seat must be left down. No hair in the sink. If he borrowed her tube of toothpaste, he'd better squeeze from the bottom. Better yet, she expected him to use his own.

Polly felt a small degree of perverse satisfaction as she read the list of rules and regulations. Normally she would never have the arrogance to demand that a guest follow such a list. Or any list, for that matter. She prided herself on having many dear friends of long standing. Reid Cameron, though, had pushed himself on her. He'd walked into her life as though he owned her and taken over. That night, he would sleep in the bedroom next to hers. She thought about it with distaste. The walls weren't soundproof.

She heard him rattling around in the cellar, doing who knew what to what. Poking into her things, her life! Grimacing, she sent her pencil racing across the paper with one last rule:

No snoring!

TWO

Reid gazed around the large, neat cellar. Cellars told a lot about people. This one blared that Polly Sweet preferred an orderly life. Everything in its proper place, nothing strewn or scattered on the floor as he'd seen in many homes. Tidy. Polly Sweet liked tidy. Plastic sheeting covered a metal clothes rack with her winter clothes. Her suitcases were lined up like bookends, near a stack of board games. Not a cobweb in sight.

Against one wall was a covered workbench, and the shelf beneath held a variety of saws and hammers. Her father's, he thought, recalling how her eyes had softened when she'd spoken of the loss of her parents. It couldn't be easy for her, living alone, responsible for the upkeep on a large piece of property and the constant repairs needed on a house and a barn. The bridge hadn't sounded sturdy to him.

He walked over to a bookcase. The titles weren't

new, indicating Ms. Sweet was also a saver. He ran his finger along one row and pulled out a black leather high school yearbook. Curious about his unwilling hostess, he flipped through it, searching for Polly Sweet's name.

Ms. Polly Sweet. Ms. Polly Sweet with the stormy blue eyes had led the debating team her senior year in high school. Ms. Polly Sweet with the luminous blue eyes had graduated at the top of her class. Ms. Polly Sweet with the spitting-angry blue eyes had been a cheerleader. A very cute cheerleader, he thought as he stared at her in her skimpy uniform. Ms. Polly Sweet's classmates had voted her Most Popular, claiming her name suited her: Sweet.

Not by a long shot! Her former classmates obviously had never seen Ms. Polly Sweet's temper!

Which she had unwisely aimed at him, instead of Grayson. He supposed it sounded farfetched to think a crook had planted stolen jewelry on her property. Grayson had, though. Ms. Polly Sweet didn't realize that once Grayson made his appearance, she'd be grateful for police protection. Therefore, whether she liked it or not, they were going to establish a working relationship.

They'd gotten off to a lousy start. He hadn't expected her to collapse at his feet with gratitude, but she'd floored him when she'd dismissed the idea of receiving a bundle in reward money. It galled him that he was stuck with a defiant writer who wouldn't take her life as seriously as her precious manuscript!

Sitting down on a metal folding chair, he absentmindedly massaged his aching thigh. The bullet that had struck him a few months earlier had nicked a nerve, temporarily paralyzing some of the sensation in his right leg. He had required intensive physical therapy before he'd regained full use and full feeling in the leg, but the leg could still ache, his personal weather barometer.

During his first week in the hospital the top brass of the state police had visited, praising him for his quick action. Not only had he stopped a bullet meant for a woman the state police had been assigned to protect, he had single-handedly arrested the shooter. At a bedside ceremony the department brass had presented him with a commendation, which he'd put in a dresser drawer in his Pittsburgh apartment, along with the other ones he'd earned.

While he'd been on leave recuperating, he had considered ending his stint with the police and putting his law degree to use. He had always known his future included practicing law, and he could see himself as a prosecuting attorney, nailing the bad guys. Still, he'd decided practicing law could wait a while longer. It wasn't as if he had a wife and children. He had never met a woman that he wanted to marry. Not enough, that is.

His former steady, the sultry Trisha of the long legs and bedroom eyes and unfaithful body had accused him of having a mistress—his police badge. Apparently she'd decided that if he could have another love, so could she. Five months after she'd moved her lingerie into his dresser drawer, he'd come home early and found her gorgeous legs locked around another man's waist. He'd tossed her, her lover, and their clothes out of his apartment. The clothes went by way of the window. Trisha had been right about one thing, he'd realized. She'd said she couldn't compete with his devotion to duty, and she couldn't.

Tough assignments suited him, and hanging out at Polly Sweet's didn't qualify as a tough assignment. Sure he'd caught a bullet and he'd been lucky, but he didn't want fear as a legacy. That was one of the reasons he'd asked his chief for a different assignment, one with more action. All his protests hadn't gotten him anywhere. So there he sat, wishing for cooperation and knowing he needed to perform a miracle upon Ms. Sweet to get it. Too bad he couldn't speak with her deceased father, get a clue on how to get through to his daughter.

He would have preferred timing his arrival to when the surveillance team tracking Grayson placed him near her home. That would mean gambling, though, and all police personnel knew the best plans often turned on a dime. While he waited for Grayson to show up, he'd make a thorough search for the jewels. If he found them, he would substitute the diamonds with cubic zirconiums. No sense letting Grayson have the advantage.

He mulled over his problem with Ms. Sweet, then smiled as an idea came to him. She didn't know it yet, but she was about to become his guide. Not only did she know her home and property, but, considering the annoyed looks he'd seen in the feisty spitfire's eyes, she'd be delighted to get rid of him by speeding the process. Which suited him fine.

He paused at the base of the staircase. He didn't hear noise coming from the kitchen. No doubt she was making good her threat with her silly list of rules. An image of her with a pencil flying over the paper had him grinning. He could think of better uses for her pouty red mouth than telling him off!

Chuckling, he recalled part of what he'd read on her computer.

His hands caressed soft flesh. Her lips tasted like fine wine. Thirsty, he lowered his head, drinking his fill.

Reid added one more fact to his store of knowledge. The not so sweet Ms. Sweet possessed one hell of a vivid imagination. In a more pleasant frame of mind he switched off the light and mounted the stairs.

"Hello," he said as he entered the kitchen.

She stood up from the table and walked over to him. "Here's your list. Kindly see it's followed."

Without even a glance he dropped the paper on the kitchen counter.

"Aren't you going to read it?"

He turned the cold-water tap on. "Mind if I have a glass of water?"

"You'll find glasses in the cabinet above your head. I want you to read my list."

He filled the glass and drank the water. "I will. I promise to read it later. Or, if you feel it's imperative, you can tell me about it while you show me around outside." He washed, dried, and returned the clean glass to where he'd found it.

She snatched the list from the Formica counter and stuck it on the refrigerator door with a magnet. "Read it!"

His voice laced with humor, he said, "You're tough." His gaze moved from the cotton top stretched across her breasts, past her rib cage, her narrow waistline, and softly curved hips, skimmed over her white shorts and down her bare legs to her white anklets and old sneakers.

"Ready, Ms. Sweet?"

"For what?" she demanded, obviously affronted at his thorough perusal.

"A walk in the sunshine. I want you to show me around."

"No, Detective Cameron, I'm not ready. Go by yourself. Take all the time you need. While you show yourself around, pretend I'm not home. I'll pretend you're not here."

As if she hadn't spoken, he took her arm, propelled her to the back door, and gave her a gentle shove outside.

"Isn't this nice?" he asked.

"It could be."

"How can you stay inside all day?" he said, determined not to let her bother him. He filled his lungs with fresh air.

"Check out this fabulous blue sky," he said. "Look

around you at the majestic mountains. The scenery is breathtaking."

She twisted free of his loose grasp. "I live here, remember? Besides, why aren't you looking at it?"

She'd caught him. "Your sour face captivates me."

"My sour face! If I look sour, it's because I'm wondering why, if you're supposedly sent to guard me, you aren't nice, polite, and respectful."

He chuckled. "That's easy. Most women in your situation would be grateful, making it simple for me to be nice, polite, and respectful."

She hooted. "Most women haven't met you. Hurling insults is not the way to get in my good graces."

"You're right. Wrong tactic. I apologize. Now, how about a truce?"

She cocked her head. "What's in it for me?"

"Why don't we find out?"

"Do I have a choice?"

"No."

"You're wrong, Detective Cameron." She turned to go.

He leaned close and said very distinctly, "Ms. Sweet, whether you are or are not interested in coming with me is immaterial to me. You will be my cooperative guide while I familiarize myself with your property. If you need an incentive to propel your feet and force polite words from your lovely viperish mouth, I suggest you think of the reward money."

She wheeled to face him, planting her hands on her

hips. "I'd rather think of how much less time you'll be here."

"Whatever works. Let's go."

As they started off, Reid inhaled the scent of spring-time in western Pennsylvania. Far more appealing than the fumes of Pittsburgh. He felt humbled by the rolling pastoral farmland, ringed by distant mountains tinted in purple and green hues.

"I see why your father chose to paint this."

Polly gazed at him, uncertain of his motives, but realizing the tough cop had a tender spot in his heart for art and nature. It made tramping over fields, wandering past a stand of apple trees, walking the line of fence posts, easier. From time to time he stopped to take his bearings, pivoting slowly until he'd looked in all directions. When she asked him why he was doing that, he replied he was mentally measuring distances from various spots to the house. He asked detailed questions, and listened intently to her replies.

"You're very thorough," she said, impressed. "We've been walking and talking for more than an hour."

"I hadn't realized." He stopped and gestured to a mound of ladybugs mating on a sycamore leaf. "Nature's grand, isn't it?" he teased.

"Terrific," she muttered.

"Lighten up."

"I was hoping we were done."

"Not a chance. It pays to be thorough. Proper

planning and preparation solves most cases. Whatever I can accomplish beforehand will help neutralize any advantage Grayson may have in coming here first."

Polly glanced at Reid. He really believed this Grayson person had hidden diamonds on her property. Despite hearing him talk about it, she couldn't fathom it. She simply couldn't take him seriously. "I still don't know how you can be certain he was here, even after all you've said."

"His whereabouts are being monitored."

"Then why haven't you arrested him?"

"We're after the big fish. Grayson's the bait. As I said, he's a member of a nasty ring of thieves. They deal in more than jewels, drugs primarily. What's over there?" He pointed across a narrow stream.

When she told him it was still her land, he took her hand without asking and helped her across the stream. When they reached the other side, she quickly freed herself.

"The boundary for my land," she said, "is on the other side of the bridge you used to get here. The state and county maintain the river that the bridge crosses."

"Do you fish?" he asked.

"I did with my dad. That is, he fished. I read a book."

She pushed her hair back from her forehead and snuck a look at him. He walked with an easy gait. His hair grew low on the back of his neck, which surprised her. Every police officer she'd ever seen wore his or her hair neat and short. Reid's longer hair defied her conception of departmental correctness. More than that, the longer she studied it, the more she was tempted to touch it, to see if it was crisp or soft, to see if the slight wave in it would curl around her fingers.

Shocked by her thoughts, she jerked her gaze away from him and desperately sought something to say.

"This area of western Pennsylvania," she began, hoping she didn't sound as flustered as she felt, "has some of the best farmland in the state. Unfortunately last May's freak late spring frost hurt the apple crop. Another boon for Washington State."

"Why do you say that? We sell plenty of apples."

"Not as many as we used to. The apples grown in the Northeast taste as good as Washington's, but you've got to give them credit. They market their apples aggressively. As a result they cornered the apple market, leaving us with a smaller share. Do you think you'll find the missing jewels?"

"I'm fairly good at getting what I'm after. So, yes, if the diamonds are here, we have high-tech ways to locate them."

"High tech?"

"Good updated, old-fashioned snooping. The insurance company's reward should ease things financially for you. A new roof must be expensive."

"It is. I saved all year for it. I'm lucky it isn't leaking over the hayloft."

She veered left, toward the river. When Reid helped her over a jagged-edge boulder, his strong hands lifting her as if she were a feather, she didn't protest. She told herself it was because she was honoring their truce, not because she liked the feel of his hands on her.

"Ms. Sweet, is there a man in your life?"

She stopped and looked at him suspiciously, ready to forget the truce. "I don't see where my private life is any of your business."

"Don't take this personally, but for the next few days everything about you is my business. Therefore, I'll ask you to answer the question."

She turned the tables on him. "Is there a woman in your life?"

He regarded her impassively. "I'm not the one in possible danger. Please answer the question."

"First tell me why you think my private life is your business."

"You're a beautiful woman." Warmth zinged through her veins, but he ruined the compliment by adding, "I don't need a jealous lover lunging at me in the dark."

"Does a scandalous liaison count?" she asked, continuing to sidestep her reply.

"You and I aren't out for a springtime stroll in the park," he said, a sarcastic edge seeping into his tone. "Yes, it counts. Any man who touches you in a familiar way counts. Do I make myself clear?"

"Very." She tossed her head. "You think your badge

entitles you to snap your fingers and make me jump through a hoop. It doesn't."

She turned her back on him and walked on. Her victory in not answering was small but significant. Anything to shake his imperious attitude.

"I'll answer personal questions," she said, "providing your partner asks them. Are you sure she's coming?"

"Yes."

"She better."

They hiked in the opposite direction from the barn, following a trail overlooking the river. With the recent rains the swiftly flowing river had risen to an unusually high level. Still, many boulders jutted upward.

Reid stared at the wooden bridge a few hundred yards away. "It sounded funny in one spot. When's the last time you had it checked for structural damage?"

"Never."

His brows knit together. "Considering that you live alone, don't you think it's wise to check it? I couldn't help noticing the wood is older than the treated kind used today. It could be rotted. How long is the bridge? About seventy feet?"

"Sixty-eight."

He nodded. "And who lives over there?" He pointed to a white bungalow with green shutters across the road.

"My aunt Martha."

He turned to her. "Keep her away."

"No," she said, shaking her head. "Don't even think about asking me to do that. In the first place it won't work. In the second place I refuse to worry her. In the third place all of this is probably for nothing. Besides, Martha comes over to see Horace."

"Who?"

"Horace, her pet milk cow."

"Are you serious?"

"Yes. Martha named her. I have a barn, so Horace lives here. You haven't seen her yet. She's out in the pasture. I'll have to bring her in soon for her radio show."

"They have shows for cows?" Reid asked, his brows raised.

"No. Martha adores Guns N' Roses, and she turned Horace on to their music. Horace refuses to give milk if she doesn't get daily doses of Axl Rose. Fortunately a local radio station loves Guns N' Roses, too, and does half-hour shows of their music three times a day. Of course, I have to rescue Cuddles before the radio turns on. His ears are too sensitive."

Reid stared at her. "Cuddles?"

"Short for Barracuda. He's another of Aunt Martha's gifts. Cuddles is a Chihuahua. Aren't you glad you dropped in?"

"My God, you're serious. I can't have your aunt coming and going as she pleases."

Polly's eyes narrowed. "I'm adamant on this. If I'm stuck with you, then you're stuck with this reality. You must have contingency plans. No one wants my aunt kept safe more than I. However, you have to admit this waiting around could be for nothing, or it could take days."

Twittering birds distracted him. He looked up to where a pair of robins sat on an overhead branch. "No, I'm certain Grayson will show. It's his mode of operation. He's under orders to produce the jewels when the higher-ups say to. Or else he's in trouble."

Polly looked out over the placid scene, then back at the hard-nosed impossible man who'd chopped off her creative juices. Worse, he showed no remorse for having ruined her afternoon.

"Despite what you say, Detective Cameron, it's supposition. My aunt Martha is not. She's real. We've always been close, but more so since my parents died. She's visiting a friend overnight, but she'll be back tomorrow. Her normal routine is that she comes over here every day to see me and her pets. Several nights a week we dine together. That way I'm assured she's eating some nutritious meals. Martha's into causes, you see. She's a member of various clubs and organizations. She reads palms and tarot cards, and casts astrological charts. She's a uniquely wonderful person, but she's not into food preparation."

"I don't care if she reads tea leaves. She stays away."

"No. I let you bully me about your staying here, since you insist Grayson's hidden the jewels here. I don't believe it, but even if I did, I won't allow you to dictate to my aunt."

She lifted her chin and refused to speak when he repeated his orders.

"All right," he almost shouted, obviously having reached the end of his patience, "then tell your aunt you're going away."

"Open your ears, Detective Cameron! I can't. Either we tell her the truth or be prepared for her visits. If I have to suffer you disrupting my life, then you must give a little. She knows I haven't planned a vacation."

"Pretend you're ill."

"Do I look ill? Aunt Martha saw me yesterday afternoon."

Once more, he made a thorough inspection of her. Her body tingled as his gaze rose up her bare legs and over her hips, lingering briefly on her breasts. When he finally reached her face, she told herself she was flushed and breathless from anger. She wasn't sure she convinced herself, though.

The corners of his mouth twitched. "Ms. Sweet, saying you're ill isn't a good idea. The fact is, you look abundantly healthy. We'll have to think of a plausible excuse."

She let out a strangled breath. The man was deliberately fractious. Hotly aware of his innuendo, she knew her skimpy attire didn't help. What she saw in his eyes, though, wasn't flirtatious foolishness, but an implacable irrevocability.

"I don't want my aunt in danger; therefore, we'll pretend you're my gardener."

"A high school boy mows your lawn once a week."

"How did you know?"

He merely raised his brows.

"Then pretend you're my plumber."

"Do you usually ask your plumber to sleep over?"

When her shoulders slumped, he suggested she pack up and visit a friend until he said she could return.

She thought of her computer, of her marvelous plans. "You're not throwing me out of my house. I'm not moving my computer, my research, all my papers, on the chance this isn't all just a wild goose chase."

"Why do I get the impression you aren't taking me seriously? Kindly remember, my job is to protect you."

"Hah! You're here to catch a thief. Who may or may not be a phantom, as far as I know. Who may or may not have hidden diamonds on my property. Your job is to 'protect me' only because I happen to be here. That's the scenario, and don't think I don't know it. *If* Grayson has been here, I'm all for letting him come back as quietly as he came the first time, take his loot, and leave. Arrest him down the road, or over in the next county. I wouldn't be the wiser."

"Are you through?" he asked in a tone that said her arguments fell on deaf ears. "If for some reason the surveillance teams report Grayson isn't coming tomorrow, Fran won't stay during the day. I will."

"Why not? What will she be doing?"

"She drew the lucky straw. She'll split her time with another case we're working on until we know Grayson is closer. It's easy to palm Fran off as your friend. But if I'm under your roof for any length of time, I need a viable reason. I'm open to suggestions."

He folded his arms, leaned back against a maple tree, and waited.

Polly bit her lower lip. What excuse could she give for having a muscular hunk in her house? She smiled and snapped her fingers. "You're my butler."

"Get serious," he drawled, giving the impression he was letting her wind down before he told her what to do.

Whatever suggestion she came up with in the next few minutes, he discounted. All for valid reasons. When she ran out of ideas, she stared mutinously at him.

Even several feet away from him, she felt his powerful impact. He was physically impressive. He spoke in a quiet, authoritative voice. Even leaning back against the tree, his thumbs tucked loosely into his pants pockets, he was not a man a woman could ignore. And that, she admitted, included herself.

"All right," she said, "if you refuse to be a gardener, a mechanic, a plumber, or anyone else I suggest, then you come up with an idea, smarty. Let's see how your creative juices work."

He was silent a moment, then straightened away from the tree. He looked into her eyes and made a suggestion that had her heart beating like a drum. Her reaction was instantaneous.

"Never!"

THREE

Reid didn't respond, he simply watched her as she went on, as if he was once again waiting for her to run out of steam.

"I may be a writer," Polly said, "but what you're asking requires an imagination even I don't possess. To pull it off, I'd need a lesson in Method acting."

His eyes darkened. "Pitching my butt on a farm with a hostile hostess isn't my idea of a heavenly assignment."

"Don't blame me. I simply can't do as you ask. You're not my type."

"You're not mine either. We're not talking marriage. We're talking about a way for me to protect you and your dotty aunt, who calls her pet milk cow Horace. A cantankerous, obstinate bovine who won't give milk unless she's listening to Guns N' Roses. And then there's Cuddles, short for Barracuda, who is not a fish but a Chihuahua!"

He kicked a stone. It sent a squirrel running. Polly realized then that he had barely been holding his temper in check.

"Why wouldn't I be delighted," he went on, "to be stuck on a farm getting bored to my eyeballs, sleeping under the same roof with an uncooperative teacher–romance novelist, who spouts how she values her time, but who, from the abundant goodness of her heart, wastes a fraction of her hallowed hour devising a stupid list of inviolate rules of behavior? Did you think I'm going to check what's on it, or do you expect me to memorize the damn thing?"

"Are you through?"

"Yes!" he thundered. "Unless I left anything out."

"One thing," she said sweetly, as she bent down to pluck a daisy.

"Which is?"

She twirled the stem beneath his nose. "Horace has a pinup poster of Axl Rose in the barn."

Reid stalked away, letting out a string of curse words that flowed back to her on the wind. He stopped abruptly, his attention caught by something at the base of tree. Following him, Polly saw a pair of possums actively mating.

"Remarkable," Reid muttered. "Wherever you look. What do you add to the water here?"

"Nothing. It's a lovely warm day in June. We're in the country. Nature is taking its course."

"Which reminds me. I omitted one thing. You're the only writer I know who has to experience a role before she writes about it."

Polly's insides were shaking, but she refused to let him see that he'd gotten a rise out of her. "I never said that. I said for me to get into the mood where you're concerned, I'd need a lesson in acting. I could, however, easily picture myself madly in love with Ashley Wilkes."

Reid scowled. "The wimp from *Gone With the Wind*?"

"Don't you dare call Ashley a wimp. He's sensitive, kind, brave, loving. Gentle. I'm sure he read poetry to Melanie."

He hooted. "Wilkes was a wimp. A wimp portrayed by Leslie Howard, a British actor who wore a pained expression on his face throughout the entire movie."

To hear Reid denigrate Ashley Wilkes sorely tested her composure, which already was marginally held together by sheer willpower. And he thought she could pretend to be his lover!

"We better settle this," he said. "What about when you acted in a school play? You used your imagination then, didn't you?"

She regarded him with impassive boredom. "For your information, the last time I acted in a school play, I was nine years old. I played a bunny rabbit. Furthermore, you can't lie about the look a woman gets in her eyes when she's in love. Other women recognize it. Sensitive men do too."

"And that is?"

"A dewy radiance. A softness. Her very soul vibrates. She longs to be alone with the man she loves. One look shared between them across a crowded room is enough to make her tingle with desire. Him, too, I might add."

"Good Lord. Is that the sort of stuff you put in your books?"

"I didn't think you'd understand. For your information it's not *stuff*. It's romance. It's what women dream of. It's obvious you don't know what I'm talking about, which says a lot about you as a lover. Not that I care. Let me put it this way, lovers are expected to want to make love. A lot. As far as I'm concerned, that lets you out."

"I'd be ecstatic to pretend we're on the verge of a nasty divorce. However, we'd first have to have been married in order for that pleasurable event to occur. May I remind you that your aunt didn't attend our wedding?"

"There is a point to this, is there not?"

"You bet there is. If you insist on letting her come here daily, she'll see me."

Polly frowned, feeling she had to come up with a workable solution. "You can hide."

"No, that's out. Now, I've tried the nice approach. It didn't work. I'm not going away. If you value your aunt's life the way I value mine, I need a logical excuse for her seeing me here. For the last time can you think of an acceptable excuse?"

"No."

"Then use mine."

"I am not enjoying this conversation, Detective Cameron."

"Neither am I, Ms. Sweet. But whether you like it or not, you're going to pretend you're in love with me. In love. The whole sloppy enchilada. Every soap opera you've seen rolled into one. Dewy radiance. Heart palpitations. If your aunt sees us together, you damn well better pretend the sun shines over my wonderful head. Bat your eyelashes like a windmill for all I care."

"I will not!"

He propped his fists on his hips. "Ms. Sweet, if you value all you say you do, then whenever your aunt Martha's around, I strongly suggest you treat me as if I'm your own personal dream Adonis!"

Her mouth open, Polly stared at him. His dark eyes glowered beneath furrowed brows. His mouth was set in a tight line.

Some Adonis!

She smiled a cool, serene smile. "Detective Cameron, you're out of your mind."

"Ms. Sweet, am I giving you the impression I'm happy?"

He looked as if he was ready to strangle her. She

lifted her chin. He lifted his. Standoff, she thought. Apparently, whatever game she played, he would too.

"Ms. Sweet, you placed this obstacle in my way. I'll give you one minute to decide. Either your aunt stays away, or you agree to my plan."

"That's not much of a choice."

"I agree." He stormed away.

Polly weighed her options. If Reid Cameron were an ordinary crazy man, she could take her shotgun and shoot him for trespassing, for forcing himself on her, for his deranged behavior. She'd find a reason to hold up in court.

Unfortunately, the Pennsylvania State Police had sent him. He represented law and order. The government. Big G. At his funeral state police from the entire nation would send uniformed mourners, representatives to honor their own. The media would take pictures of their black armbands. Cameron's likeness on TV would taunt her. What support would she have? She knew the board of education wouldn't approve of a kindergarten teacher–murderer.

She stole a glance at him, and a shiver ran through her. He stood on a rise overlooking the river, one leg bent, the foot resting on a rock. His hand was absently rubbing the thigh. From this distance he looked formidable.

She was back to square one, between a rock and a hard place. If she told Martha not to come, she'd distress her aunt. Martha had had a minor heart scare last year. Polly wasn't going to do anything to push it into the major column.

If she visited Martha instead, Martha wouldn't see Horace, and that would distress both her aunt and the cow. With a miserable sense of inevitability, Polly realized that much as she'd like to tell Cameron to take a flying leap off that bluff, she couldn't.

He was right. Arguing was silly if it endangered Martha. And her aunt, bless her heart, thrived on gossip. The telephone grew out of her ear. With her vast circle of friends, each would know within the day that a lawman was camped out in her niece's house. Then, too, what if one of her own friends dropped in?

She was about to go to Reid and surrender, so to speak, when he turned and walked back to her.

"Time's up," he said. "Suppose we rehearse."

She blinked. "Rehearse?"

He rubbed the back of his neck. "You pretend I'm Ashley. I'll try fooling myself into thinking you're Scarlett. One kiss ought to do it. Consider it your Method acting lesson."

She laughed outright. "Oh, that's rich. Actually it's sickening. What a line! Let me get this perfectly clear. You want to kiss me—"

He slammed one fist into the other hand. "No. I don't want to kiss you. I want to catch a thief. I want to leave faster than you want me to. But we need to convince your aunt and Grayson I'm here for personal reasons. So consider this your acting lesson,

Ms. Sweet. See if you can manage to get the glazed look in your eyes you claim lovers share."

She poked his chest. Her finger hit brick. "Wait! Aunt Martha won't be home until tomorrow evening. You could be gone by then. Grayson might not see me."

"I can't chance it. Not with her, not with Grayson. He's not calling me on the phone to let me know his exact time of arrival. Suppose he sees us?"

"So?"

"I enjoy living. I need a cover too!"

"Don't yell at me. Suppose the worst happens, and I'm stuck with you for a few days? Then how do I explain your sleeping here to my aunt?"

He shrugged. "Let her think we're resuming an old love affair. Or let her think I'm a new man in your life. I don't care what you tell her as long as you make it convincing."

Polly muttered an impolite word under her breath. "All right. Get it over with."

Reid put his hands on her shoulders. She puckered her lips, squeezed her eyes shut, and shuddered.

"What are you doing?"

Her eyes popped open. He'd cocked his head and was frowning with puzzlement.

"Getting ready," she said tartly.

His mouth pulled into a sour line to match hers. "Getting ready? How do you expect me to pretend you're Scarlett when you purse your lips like some damn fish? And what's with this shivering and scrunching your eyes? Is that how you kiss a man?"

She didn't bother to respond. Anxious to get it over with, she raised up on tiptoes, brushed her lips across his cheek, and stepped back.

"There," she said. "The Method acting class is over. Thank you for your edifying lesson. I've never had a more illuminating kiss, or one that left me hotter. Now, if you'll excuse me, Detective Cameron, it's nearing dinner. I'm eating light tonight. A tuna sandwich and iced tea. I don't suppose you want a sandwich?"

Without waiting for his answer, she whipped off in the other direction. She hadn't gotten ten steps before his ominous, silky voice rang out.

"Aren't you forgetting something, Ms. Sweet?"

She swiveled. "Sorry. What kind of bread do you like?"

"Come back here. We're not through."

"Really?" she said airily. "I am."

"Stop acting as if you're writing a scene for your book. I'm serious." He walked toward her, stopping less than two feet away. "You said a woman gets a certain look in her eyes. Whatever it is, you look the same as you did before. You wouldn't fool anyone into thinking we're lovers."

She could feel his sharp eyes issue a challenge. Allowing Martha to visit was her idea. Now he was daring her to go through with their agreed-upon plan.

There was a hint of coiled restraint about the way he stood, his feet apart, his hands at his waist, pushing his jacket back. There wasn't an ounce of fat on his lanky frame. He was a big man, in height and, she suspected, in strength. He also was obviously a man used to getting his way.

She blew a lock of hair from her face. "Why do we need to rehearse? If Grayson comes here, I guarantee you I won't be thinking about a lover. The look on my face will be fright."

Reid raised his head skyward as if willing God to give him strength to deal with her.

"But," he said, "this still leaves us with Aunt Martha's daily visit. Unless you tell her to keep away, you have to convince your aunt we're lovers. Which means you need another lesson. I hope this is the last."

Before Polly registered his eyes were hotter than coals, before she could utter a whimper of protest, he yanked her to him, cradled her head so that she couldn't move, and kissed her. She opened her mouth to demand he stop, but he boldly swept his tongue inside, and with a ruthless possession, explored her mouth.

Polly was in shock. His warm breath mingled with hers. Spreading his legs a bit, he aligned their bodies, then he placed his hands on her hips, bringing her forward. Aware of all of him, she knew she should slap his face, or lift her knee for a well-aimed jab, but she couldn't. Instead, she kissed him back.

Texture and taste melded. His hands slid over her buttocks, held her to him. Then he suddenly lifted his head. His astonished breath hissed from him, as if he too, were experiencing an instant shock.

"Damn," he muttered, shaking his head slowly. "Ms. Sweet, you're one hell of a big surprise. Who expected this?"

She tried to speak, but she didn't know what to say. He didn't give her the chance anyhow. He lowered his head and began kissing her again, pressing his hips forward at the same time.

The heady kiss sent liquid heat coursing through her to the pit of her stomach. Surprise. He'd called her a surprise. That was mild compared to how she felt about him at that moment. Her heart did a little flip-flop, then a series of somersaults.

Slipping her hands around his neck, she threaded her fingers through his thick hair. She was aware of the steady beating of his heart and knew the second its speed matched hers. She clung to him, searching her brain for the perfect excuse to be answering his kisses.

Research, she thought disjointedly. The rational idea of gathering research for her romance books settled her mind as she arched her neck provocatively. He growled low in his throat, then kissed her neck. When she purred, he left a hot trail of kisses on her face, her eyes, her cheeks. His hands roamed from hip to rib cage, then downward to touch and knead the bare flesh of her thighs, as if assuring himself of her feminine curves.

Polly was flabbergasted by the amount of research she was getting for her novels. Detective Cameron kissed the way the hero of a hot romance book should kiss. He pulled her roughly to him and planted a tantalizing kiss on the sensitive spot at the base of her throat. For herself, she would always prefer a tamer man, a caring man who asked, never a macho type who took. But, she thought, pulling Reid's head back up for another soul-shattering kiss, if this man succeeded in sending poor Ashley to second place this fast, it proved just how paltry her love scenes had been. No wonder she'd received five rejection letters. Each editor had said her love scenes needed more punch.

She mated her tongue with his. She molded her body to his. Excusing her wanton behavior, she promised to describe the stirring sensation in her next love scene. She wiggled closer, marveling at the way his muscular arms enfolded her. At the way his thighs cradled her. At the way his hard body quivered with life. How wonderful for the opportunity to investigate Reid Cameron's masterful method of seduction. All in the name of gathering research.

Reid wasn't gathering anything in the name of research. He was hoarding moments of exquisite, unexpected pleasure. Somewhere in his fogged-up brain, his conscience reared up to mock him. He knew damned well what had prompted him to silence her sassy mouth. She had driven him up the wall, then refused to listen to reason. With her nonsense about needing a Method acting lesson, he'd decided to show her.

Only his scheme had backfired. Who was giving whom the lesson? He wasn't kissing her to save old aunt what's her name's life in case she dropped in when Grayson made his appearance. He wasn't even kissing her to fool Grayson or the aunt into thinking he was her lover. He was kissing Polly Sweet for purely selfish reasons.

One he could get fired for in a shot.

Hell! He deserved to be fired for it.

He kissed her incredible mouth with a ferocity that didn't begin to calm his desire. He now knew how it felt to be hit by a Mack truck speeding out of control down a steep incline.

And speeding out of control was exactly what was happening to him. Exerting more willpower than he'd thought he'd need, he softened the kiss. It was light and heady and, oddly, much more potent. Knowing he had to stop now or let nature take its course, he reluctantly ended the kiss. Cradling her face in his hands, he gazed down at her.

Her breathing was ragged, and her cheeks were flushed with passion. She dropped her hands from his neck and opened her eyes. They were languorous, dewy, and she stared at him as if she were waiting for him to explain the mind-boggling kisses they'd shared. His gaze dropped to her lips. They were swollen from his kisses, and as he watched, she dragged her tongue across them. He ruthlessly suppressed the hot urges of his body. A man knew when a woman's needs matched his. He and his reluctant pupil would be good together. Better than good. Dynamite. How dare she do this to him? He was stunned by the craving he felt. He knew instinctively that on some deep level they were connected. Almost as if their meeting had been preordained.

Stop! Warning bells rang in his head. The wisest—the only acceptable—course of action for him was to remain focused on his mission. Get in. Get out. Minimize risks. Leave no emotional trails. He steeled himself against temptation, against her beckoning rosebud lips.

Hiding his internal struggle, he slapped a grin on his face.

"I think you've got the dewy look you were aiming for. If I meet your aunt Martha, remember what we did to get it there. It's on your head if she knows too much."

Polly flinched, the sensual haze that surrounded her shattered by his callous words. Her voice trembled, but she managed to speak through her humiliation.

"Detective Cameron, I had my own reason for kissing you back. I was gathering research for my book."

His grin only broadened. "I'm sure we could research ourselves into having a great time with a mattress beneath us, but I'm not here to help you with your writing. I'll have tuna on rye. If you don't have rye, white's fine. Not too much mayo, I'm watching my figure."

Berating herself, she spun on her heels, putting as much distance between them as fast as humanly possible. She didn't want him seeing the tears brimming in her eyes. Idiot! she scolded herself. Was her life so barren, she would kiss a man she didn't like?

She fled to the pasture. Horace lifted her head, mooing as Polly approached. "Come on, girl. It's lovely outside, and you want to stay here, but I'm stuck with unwanted guests, so in you go."

Horace didn't care for her excuse. Polly coaxed the cow into the barn, leading her past the wooden barrels she'd set around to catch the water from the leaky roof.

Cuddles lay snoring on a tiny mound of hay. The dog and cow were great friends, and Cuddles often trotted into the barn to visit Horace. But he disliked the pasture, so he would sleep inside while Horace was out. Polly lifted the sleeping dog up in her arms. In a few minutes the portable radio on the shelf would click on for the evening Guns N' Roses show. That would settle Horace down for the night. She'd tried the Grateful Dead and Bon Jovi, but Horace was strictly a Rose fan.

Cuddles snuggled in her arms. Routines, she

thought, kissing his soft neck. Nice, dependable routines. Far better for her emotional well-being than Reid Cameron coaxing a lovesick look into her eyes by kissing the socks off her.

She carried the dog inside the house and put him in the basket she kept for him in the laundry room. Glancing at her watch, she saw it was almost six o'clock. Good grief! Where had the day gone?

She had just entered the kitchen to make dinner when she heard a car out front. Walking to the front door, she saw a tall blond woman getting out of a gray station wagon. She wore tan slacks and an attractive cotton sweater.

Stepping outside, Polly introduced herself, thinking Reid's partner was one of the prettiest women she'd ever seen.

Fran smiled warmly at her. "I'm Fran Mohr, Reid's partner. I'm sure he's explained the operation. You can feel safe with us. We're a good team."

"He mentioned it."

"I jabber. He's the strong, silent type, but we're both dedicated to protecting you."

"What a great place," Fran went on, admiring the two-story white farmhouse. The shutters were Wedgwood blue, and brass carriage lamps hung on either side of the tall oak door. A wide veranda ran along the front of the house, and sitting on it were redwood tubs of showy white, red, yellow, and purple petunias and blue-and-white wicker rockers.

"You have a fabulous view of the Allegheny Mountains," Fran added. "It's so quiet, too, not like Pittsburgh, where I live." A smile lit her warm hazel eyes. "I hope you don't mind my sharing your bedroom. It will only be for a short while."

She turned back to the car. "I stopped at the supermarket, and I took a chance that you own a large refrigerator. We don't want you to worry about feeding us. We'll try not to disturb you too much. We'll clean up, make our beds, make sure there's no hairs in the bathroom sink."

On her first trip into the kitchen toting the bags of food Fran had bought, Polly snatched the list of rules she'd made off the refrigerator and tossed it into the garbage pail.

"Have you and Detective Cameron been partners long?" she asked when she and Fran had finished carrying in the groceries.

"About two years. He's terrific, really wonderful. I trust him with my life. The women in the office are nuts about him. I'm regularly pestered to put in a good word for them."

"Do you?" Polly asked, curious as to the extent of their relationship.

"No. Reid and I prefer keeping our private lives separate from work. Did he tell you I'm going to be working on another case until we know Grayson's nearby?"

"Yes," Polly replied. Apparently Fran and her partner were a hot item, which made his kissing her an awful thing to do.

"I bought a variety of foods," Fran said as she started unloading the bags. "I'm a good cook. Ask Reid. If you like, I'll make dinner tonight."

"Be my guest, although I was just going to have a tuna fish sandwich. You will be here at night, won't you?"

"Of course. And before it gets dark tonight, I'd like to familiarize myself with your house and grounds."

Fran's bubbly nature was contagious, and Polly quickly decided she liked her. While Fran chatted, she opened two cans of tuna and chopped some celery, then let Fran take over while she made iced tea.

"I add a dash of relish for zest," Fran said. "Mustard or lemon works as well. The trick is to control the amount. Reid prefers his tuna with lemon."

Fran sliced a lemon. "He's okay in the kitchen, but I'm better. Some things we like to do together."

Polly easily imagined what those things were. It was clear the two maintained a close, perhaps intimate, relationship. With dinner under control she excused herself and went into the den to shut off her computer. When she looked up, Reid was lounging casually against the jamb.

She felt a tremor of excitement, as if he were dwarfing the room with his size, pulling her toward him. "Your partner is very nice."

"I'm glad you like her."

"I'm sure you do too."

He stared at Polly's mouth. "I do, very much. She's a highly capable professional. She has a wonderful sense of humor. Best of all, she's agreeable."

"She's so agreeable, she's fixing your tuna the way you like it."

"How's that?" he asked.

His unruffled demeanor strained hers. "With lemon."

"Tell me, Ms. Sweet, what would you have put in my tuna?"

"Poison."

He chuckled. "I thought so."

"Detective Cameron, are you deliberately trying to get my goat?"

A half-grin lifted one corner of his mouth. "Is that what I'm doing?"

"You're trying to."

"Am I succeeding?"

"Of course not!"

"Did you enjoy the kiss?"

Very much. Too much. "Don't be silly!"

"It bothers me to say I did."

"Then consider it research. I am."

He scowled. "So that's what you're still telling yourself?"

She swallowed. "Naturally. What else could it be?"

"Beats me." Suddenly his scowl switched to a smile. "But I'm a true proponent of educational research." He pushed away from the doorjamb and started toward her. Slowly and boldly, his gaze slid down over her body, before rising again and focusing on her eyes with a sizzling look.

"So, Ms. Sweet," he drawled, "let's see if practice makes perfect. In the name of research. Naturally."

FOUR

Reid kicked the door shut.

Polly gulped. "This is my sanctuary. I'd appreciate it if you'd knock first."

"I will. Next time."

"See that—"

He cupped her face. "Next time." His kiss silenced her. His mouth was hotter, wetter, a more deliberate sensual trap than before.

She was shaking when he released her.

"Why did you do that?" she demanded.

"I wanted to see if kissing you elicited the same response it had before. It did. I'm beginning to get used to that look in your eyes. Coming?" he asked, opening the door.

She pushed past him in a regal huff. He was vile, she thought, fuming. Why had she responded to his kiss a second time? More research, she told herself, but how dare he bait her? She was getting angrier by the second. She swore she wouldn't give him the satisfaction of letting him know how much he bothered her. Especially with Fran waiting.

In the kitchen Reid greeted Fran warmly. He then led her toward the front of the house, leaving Polly alone for a long while. She presumed they were either updating each other on their cases, or they were sharing an extended kiss hello. Damn him. He was alarmingly sexy. Little wonder the women in his office panted for him. But not her. She was on to him. A man like him could never be for her.

If it weren't for her need to gather research for her novels, she would never be able to explain her outrageous behavior. In all her life she had never acted so brazenly. On the other hand their fiery kisses didn't appear to have affected him. She supposed she ought to be grateful he hadn't made a big deal out of it. If he had, he would have made it impossible for her to talk to him, let alone have him sleep in her home.

Her friends Grace, Joan, and Lonni would be amazed if they knew what had transpired between her and the state trooper. She'd never tell them, though. They couldn't understand her fixation with Ashley Wilkes instead of Rhett Butler.

"What does that placid man do for your juices?" they asked.

Not much, Polly realized. She had been hot for the lawman. Annoyed at the thought, she filled a glass with cold water and was finishing drinking it just as he strolled back into the kitchen.

"Are you all right?" he asked, leaning close to her. "Your face is flushed."

"I'm fine. Let's eat."

The three sat at the kitchen table, Reid across from her. "I asked Fran's opinion about your bridge. She agrees with me. It needs to be checked."

"My bridge is sturdy, Detective Cameron. I'm certain what you both heard are normal creaks from expansion and contraction. Wood breathes."

"I'll check it anyway," Reid said.

Polly didn't answer, using the excuse of eating as a reason to remain quiet. She was a bundle of nerves. More than once, she caught Reid's hawklike gaze on her, and she was thankful when Fran drew her into the conversation. A half hour of pleasant conversation flew by as Fran talked about her Victorian doll collection and Polly recounted several stories about her students' funnier antics.

"I could never be a teacher," Fran said.

"I love kids. I could never be a police officer."

"Fran," Reid said, "Ms. Sweet disapproves of our tactics."

Polly turned to Reid. Her heart was beating so loud, it was a wonder he couldn't hear it, or that Fran didn't sense the tension between them.

"*Your* tactics, Detective Cameron. I can't judge

anyone else's in the Pennsylvania State Police, only yours."

His eyes narrowed. "Is that so? Then you ought to know that sometimes my tactics switch. Sometimes they depend on the hand I'm dealt."

"Sometimes," she said, "the game is so new, the rules are hard to understand."

He leaned forward. "That's why it's better to discuss the rules in a civilized manner. Then again, things can get out of hand when people allow their emotions to get in the way."

Polly grimaced. "Which should remind a woman to stay on guard, lest an unwelcome situation arises. Wouldn't you agree?"

"Definitely. Although sometimes a woman isn't honest about her feelings. When she lets go, it stuns her. The man too."

Fran's gaze was shifting from one to the other. "What's going on?" she asked. "Am I missing something I should know?"

Polly dropped a clenched hand from the table to her lap. With effort she broke eye contact with Reid and looked at Fran.

"What Detective Cameron means, Fran, is that when he first explained his reason for coming here, I didn't believe him. I asked him to leave. Repeatedly."

Fran turned to Reid, eyebrows raised. "That's new for you, isn't it, Reid? Most women take what you say as the gospel."

"Not Ms. Sweet."

"I wasn't gracious," Polly continued. "I resented him interfering with my work. I still do. He has a way of forcing his opinions on a person. My summer break is very important to me. It's a time when I can write without interruption. But," she sighed resignedly, "now that I understand he won't leave without arresting Grayson, I'll do whatever I can to help."

Fran nodded. "From your perspective I can understand our presence is difficult to accept."

"I don't mean you, Fran." She flashed an angry look at Reid. "Detective Cameron came into my den before dinner to remind me of my role."

Fran dabbed her mouth with her napkin. "As long as we're going to be together for a while, shouldn't you two call each other by first names?"

"That's fine with me, Polly," Reid said. "Especially under the circumstances."

Polly inclined her head. Once again, she was stuck between a rock and a hard place. If she refused, Fran would become suspicious. "Me too, *Reid*."

Reid scowled as Polly angled her chair away from the table, presenting him with her profile. She folded her arms over her chest, which only made him more aware of her breasts, and crossed one leg over the other. Despite himself, his gaze fixed on the smooth bare flesh of her thigh. How dare she pretend he didn't exist? Pretend that kiss in the den hadn't been dynamite!

He suppressed a wild urge to lift her from her chair and give her a firm talking-to. He'd invested a lot of hard work and many years building his career. He comforted himself that in a week or two, he'd forget he met her.

Turning to Fran, he told her about Polly's aunt. By the time Fran heard the list of her interests, learned she lived across the road and stopped by daily, she grew concerned.

"Don't worry," Reid said. "Polly and I worked it out. To minimize the risk, and should Grayson slip through our net and see Polly with me, we're going to pretend we're involved."

"In what?" Fran asked.

"A romance."

Fran choked politely. "You two?" She looked at them both with obvious doubt. "Do you think it will work?"

Reid shrugged. "It's the only gimmick I could come up with that might keep her aunt from gossiping that the police are staying here."

"I'm hoping Grayson comes and goes before my aunt returns tomorrow," Polly said.

"It's novel, I must say. What made you think of that, Reid?"

"I got the idea from the romance book Polly's writing."

Fran turned to Polly. "If you have to be convincing, do you think you can pull this off?"

"What Fran is asking," Reid said, his tone casual, "is, are you willing to kiss me in front of your aunt?"

Polly stood and carried her dishes to the sink. It took all her willpower not to smash them, to respond in a calm voice.

"Only if absolutely necessary, and only if you remember it's an act."

"Naturally."

He managed to fill that one word with all sorts of innuendo, and she turned to glare at him. Her attention was caught, however, by Cuddles padding into the kitchen, heading straight for Reid.

"Watch out!" she said. "My dog's right under your foot."

Reid's head shot down. "What the—?"

Cuddles was short-coated, with overly large ears, soulful chocolate-brown eyes, and a little tail that spun like a top. The dog climbed onto Reid's sneaker, heaved a sigh from its exertions, then lifted his face to stare at Reid.

Reid threw back his head and roared. "I take it this is your guard dog."

Polly snatched Cuddles from Reid's shoe. She held the dog high, giving it a playful shake. "Meet Barracuda. Cuddles, for short. The way he acts, you can see why we call him Cuddles."

She explained to Fran that her aunt had presented him as a watchdog. "Translated, that means his mother had another litter. Cuddles was jealous, so I inherited him."

She handed the wiggling dog over to Reid. It promptly transferred its affection, lavishly licking his face. Reid ducked when it aimed its tongue at his mouth.

"Some watchdog," he said. "I noticed that you keep your doors unlocked. You invite burglars, then you expect this pip-squeak to protect you."

Cuddles aimed another lick. Reid chuckled and scratched the dog's warm belly, setting off another round of mad tail wagging. Polly smiled as she watched. When Reid handed the dog back to her, their eyes met. They both had been laughing at Cuddles's antics, but now their smiles vanished. As Reid gazed at her speculatively, she watched the intriguing play of emotions on his face. Her cheeks warmed, and she was the first to break their eye contact.

She cleared her throat. "Come on, Cuddles, down you go."

Reid cleared the rest of the dishes from the table. He and Fran loaded the dishwasher while Polly wiped off the counters and table.

"Thanks for the meal," he said to Polly. "Fran, you're handling the checkbook. Please compensate Polly for whatever we use. She shouldn't pay the state's bill."

"It's okay," Polly said. "Fran brought groceries."

Reid nodded. "Now that we've got that settled." He opened the back door. "Polly, I'd like to talk with you, please."

She heard the change in his voice. He was asking, not demanding. Still, she hesitated. "Can't it wait? I planned to work for a while, to make up for lost time."

He held out his hand. "Please."

When she couldn't think of another reason to delay, she followed him outside.

They walked across the yard to where a small bench sat beneath an oak tree. They both sat, their shoulders touching. Polly heard him sigh, then he picked up her hand, almost as if he didn't want to but was afraid she'd bolt otherwise.

"Polly, there's something I want to say to you, without Fran hearing."

She was acutely conscious of her hand in his, of his hard thigh pressing her bare leg.

"I didn't mean to step out of line. We need to discuss that kiss if we're going to work together." His grip tightened.

"I'd rather not."

He nodded. "Then I will. I don't push myself on women. Also, I appreciate how much your writing means to you. If I've given you the wrong impression, I'm sorry."

She looked at him and saw he was serious.

"I meant what I said about your dad's talent too," he added. "It wasn't a ploy to get you to cooperate with me."

She smiled and relaxed back on the bench. It was nice, she decided, holding hands with him. Not threatening in the least. "I know. You couldn't hide what I saw in your eyes, heard in your voice when you spoke about his paintings."

"Then I'm not all bad?" he teased.

"No." He was dangerous, she thought, feeling heat emanating from his body. Dangerous, but not bad.

"Truce? Again?"

She looked up at him, surprised to see his head so close to hers. If she moved just an inch this way, and he moved just an inch that way, their lips would meet. She was tempted, strongly tempted, to move that inch, but her common sense reasserted itself just in time.

"Truce," she murmured, drawing back from him. "I hope you catch Grayson," she added.

"We will. It's only a question of time."

They sat in silence for several minutes, enjoying the evening quiet, then he asked, "Do you like living alone?"

"I'm never totally alone. I have my job, which keeps me busy, my aunt, and my animals."

Reid studied her. He could smell a nonanswer a mile away. He wondered about her love life, but held his counsel. If he opened that can of worms, he'd lose her goodwill, which, he realized, he wanted very much.

"Sitting here," he said, "it's hard to visualize the ugly underbelly of life that I see all the time. It's easy to see why living in the country suits you."

"Did you always want to be in law enforcement?"

"Yes, for the present. No, for the long term. I have a law degree. When I tire of this, I'll put it to good use."

She nodded. "What does Fran think about your plans? It affects her too."

He shrugged. "I guess Frannie's supportive."

"You don't know?"

Polly was shocked. If she were intimately involved with Reid, she'd give him her wholehearted support in starting a law practice. Surely a life outside of the line of fire was preferable to packing a gun, living in constant danger. Then again, Fran had chosen the same profession as Reid.

"I'm sure she's supportive," Reid said. "Fran's a terrific woman."

Polly told herself it made no sense to get involved in his and Fran's private affairs. He'd apologized for any misinterpretation about his kiss, which ended it as far as she was concerned.

She stood abruptly. "If that's all you wanted to talk about, I'll leave you and Fran to do whatever you do."

He walked alongside her to the house. "Don't worry," he said, apparently interpreting her sudden mood shift as concern about Grayson. "I won't let anything happen to you."

Inside the house Polly went straight to her den, but

she couldn't concentrate on her writing. After an hour of fiddling, she called it a night.

She found Fran and Reid playing a fast game of double solitaire in the living room. The TV was on. Cuddles sat on Reid's lap, acting as if he owned Reid. Polly joined them. When the *Tonight* program ended, they decided to go to bed.

Polly invited Fran to use the bathroom first, then Reid. Fran didn't loiter. Within minutes she was back in Polly's bedroom, saying good night as she crawled into her bed.

Polly undressed. Wearing her pink shortie nightgown, she waited for what she thought was a decent length of time. Not hearing Reid, she padded into the bathroom, washed her face and brushed her teeth, and walked back out into the hall.

And straight into Reid. His shirt was open, giving her a free view of his broad chest. As his gaze flashed over her body, her nerve endings flashed danger signals. Thinking she was safe, she hadn't bothered with her robe. It hung in her closet, but the closet door squealed, and she hadn't wanted to disturb Fran. She should have, she thought as she saw Reid's eyes darken with passion. And she really wished he hadn't unbuttoned his shirt.

"Excuse me," she said, flustered. The hallway suddenly seemed steamy, close. She moistened her lips. "My robe . . . Fran's sleeping. The closet door squeaks, and I didn't want to disturb her. I thought you were through in the bathroom."

"I was waiting for you to finish first."

"Oh. Well, I'm done. Good night."

As if rooted to the spot, each waited for the other to make the first move. As if in slow motion, Reid reached out and lifted a lock of her hair, letting it sift through his fingers. She held her breath.

His hand lowered to her shoulder, almost completely bared by the scoop neck of her nightgown. The feel of his warm skin on hers jolted her back to reality. And reality was that he would only be in her home for a few days while he did his job.

"Please let me pass," she said. "We should get a good night's sleep."

Nodding, he stepped back. "Good night, Polly. Sweet dreams."

She smiled fleetingly at the small joke he'd made with her name, then slipped around him, heading for her bedroom. As she shut her door, she wondered if she'd only imagined him whispering after her, "For my dreams will certainly be sweet."

As early as Polly rose to milk Horace, she found Fran's bed empty, the aroma of coffee wafting up the stairs. She dressed quickly in shorts and a sleeveless blouse and went downstairs to the kitchen. Reid was sitting on a chair, with Cuddles riding on his shoe.

"Good morning," Reid said. "How did you sleep?"

"Like a log. Where's Fran?"

He put Cuddles on the floor and stood. "She's out walking. And I can tell you didn't sleep any better than I did."

His voice sounded so intimate, it quickened her heartbeat. "Then why did you ask?"

"I wanted to see if you're as truthful as I am. You're not."

Their eyes met and held. Goose bumps rose on her flesh. She had the answer to the tormenting question that had kept her up long into the night. She hadn't imagined the strong sexual pull between them. If she just steered clear of him, she told herself, everything would be fine.

She asked what he wanted for breakfast, but he said breakfast was on him.

"We're going out?" she asked, surprised.

"No, I'm on duty. I'm the official breakfast cook."

The specter of Grayson loomed before her.

"Yes, of course," she said, wishing her emotions weren't running so high, wishing he wouldn't watch her so intently. "I'd love whatever you're fixing. Should we wait for Fran? I'm lucky the rain held up last night. It should help dry out the barn before the predicted deluge."

She turned away in embarrassment as Reid grinned at her. She'd never babbled in her life. What was it about this man that made her act so out of character?

Deciding a tactical retreat was in order, she headed for the barn to milk Horace.

During breakfast Fran reported that she had phoned headquarters. Grayson wasn't expected to show up until Monday. They'd learned from the tap on his phone that he'd decided to spend the weekend in Ohio at his girlfriend's.

Polly treated the news as a mixed bag. It meant another night with Reid sleeping in the next bedroom, and her aunt would definitely meet him.

After they'd cleaned up the breakfast dishes, Reid walked to the back door. He paused there, his hand on the knob, and casually said to Polly, "I'm sorry about making you change your plans again today. I'd like to search the barn for the jewels. Could you meet me there in, say, half an hour?"

She was stunned, and she stared at the screen door for a full minute after he'd left. She'd planned on writing that day. She hadn't planned on searching the barn with Reid. Was he crazy? Even if she hadn't anticipated finishing the love scene he'd interrupted the day before, the barn was the last place she wanted to be with him. Barns had haylofts, and she knew what the hero in her book would do with the heroine in a hayloft.

Alarmed, she ran outside and caught up with him. "I don't see why I should poke around the hayloft too. Maybe you have nothing else to do, but I do. Doesn't my work count?"

He kept walking. There was no use arguing with him. He didn't put her romance novel on an equal par with his work. Men! she thought. Had she been writing a thesis on devious-minded criminals, or just plain devious-minded men, or one stubborn Pennsylvania state trooper whose initials were R.C., she bet she'd get his serious attention.

"Reid, did you hear me?"

He stopped and faced her. "Who wouldn't? I know what you're thinking, but you're way off base. I thought we cleared everything up last night."

She clenched and unclenched her fists, mumbled under her breath, then opened her mouth.

"Don't say it," he told her, walking back to her. "You'll do me an enormous favor if you stopped grumbling. Think ahead to the time when Fran and I will be gone. It'll come sooner than you realize. In the meantime please accept the fact that we're tied to each other for the duration. And don't bother telling me you'd rather be tied to Ashley Wilkes. I already know that." He glanced behind her toward the house. "And if you're smart, you'll keep from flying off the handle with me in front of Fran. Otherwise, she'll think there's something going on between us."

Polly pulled herself up tall. The insufferable man was too blasted close. "We wouldn't want that, would we? Not considering your relationship with Fran."

"Fran? Fran Mohr?" His brows and his voice rose.

Exasperated, she said, "How many Frans do you know? Yes, Fran Mohr."

He set his hands on his hops. "Frannie's a friend and a partner."

"She's your—your . . . girlfriend."

If possible, his eyebrows rose even higher. "Did she tell you that?"

"Not in so many words. She admitted she likes working with you more than any man she knows."

Reid grinned. The tension eased off his shoulders. Polly had the distinct impression she was providing his morning's entertainment.

"Fran Mohr is a fine woman," he said. "A true professional. I hate to bust your romance novelist's plot line, but I'm serving as best man at her wedding next month. She's marrying a buddy of mine, Tom Meredith. Frannie thinks everyone should be married. I don't. Her wedding is as close to the altar as I care to get."

He wasn't marrying Fran. It pleased her to know he hadn't come on to her while in love with another woman. "Scared of women?" she teased.

He rested his hands on her shoulders and gave her a smile so full of blatant sex appeal, it could light a city. His gaze drifted to her lips. "Last night, Polly, did I give you the impression I'm scared of you?"

"Don't bring up last night. If you're trying to earn points as the macho man of the century, I'll give you five. Which doesn't stop me from thinking you're afraid of a commitment."

His smile switched to a scowl. The air between them was ripe with sexual tension. Her eyes blazed, her lips beckoned. Cursed with knowing her taste, he wanted to kiss the smirk off her ruby-red lips.

"Put it this way," he said, his tone stretched taut as a guy wire. "When I want unnecessary prattle, I'll find a woman like you and get married!"

She hooted, shrugging his hands off her shoulders. "Don't flatter yourself. I wouldn't marry a cynical cop like you if you were the last man on earth."

He gave a harsh, humorless laugh. "Don't push me, Polly. Get your kicks writing your romance novel."

"If you're implying writing romance fills my lonely life, you're wrong. I have a date tonight."

That was a lie. She didn't have a date. But if she had to sit in the nearby town's one movie theater and see the picture three times, she'd do it, anything rather than let Reid think she hid from life behind her computer.

"Break your date. You're staying here."

"I will not!"

He shoved his hands into his pockets. "What were you going to do?"

"Horizontally or vertically?" she asked sweetly.

His glare became frigid, and she decided it would be wise to stop the teasing.

"Our usual," she said. "Dining and dancing."

"Where?"

"Wherever we please. We don't live in the boon-docks. There are places in town. What kind of inquisition is this?"

"You're right," he said. "I apologize. Nevertheless, you're well known in the community. Therefore, the chances are fairly high you'll be recognized. Won't it look odd if you're falling all over one man while you're in love with another?"

"But I'm not in love," she said, giving him a sincere but baffled look.

He trailed his thumb across her lower lip. She slapped his hand away. His mouth twisted in a wry smile.

"So excitable," he murmured. "Have you forgotten so soon? You're madly in love with me. And don't tell me you didn't feel what I did when we kissed, because I know better."

Her eyes widened in shock at his arrogance. He just smiled at her. "I'll try to control myself when we get up to the hayloft," he said.

She half expected him to kiss her again, but he didn't. She was furious with herself for feeling disappointed. It didn't take a rocket scientist to know that whatever she might think of him personally, her body wasn't listening.

As she walked beside him to the barn, she decided

that sparring with Reid Cameron was a no-win fight. The best thing to do was help him find the damn jewels, so he would leave her alone. Midway to the barn, she heard the radio playing. Stopping, she glanced at her watch and frowned.

Reid wheeled around. "What's wrong?"

She bit her lip. "It's odd. I'm positive I reset the timer this morning. I left Horace in the barn after I milked her so she could hear her program. The station moved it up an hour. That's why I changed the timer, but the radio should have shut off by now."

Reid's gaze swept the grounds, taking in the barn, the field, and following the line of fence posts. Nothing struck him as out of the ordinary, and he was confident that the surveillance team's information about Grayson being in Ohio was accurate. He looked back at Polly. "You probably set it wrong."

"I guess," she muttered. She walked alongside him for a few steps, then grabbed his hand. "Ohmigod! I just thought of a horrible reason why the radio is on. Grayson might be in the barn. It's conceivable he switched off the radio while we were eating breakfast. Horace would get so upset she'd make a racket. Grayson would turn the radio back on rather than chance our hearing Horace's fussing."

Reid marveled at her accurate deductions, but he was more concerned at calming her than worrying about Grayson.

"I doubt if he's in the barn. You heard Fran say

he's miles away, but just to make sure, I'll check. You walk, don't run, back to the house. Tell Fran what's going on."

Panic seized her. "I can't."

He searched her face. He could take her anger at him—he'd asked for it, pushing her the way he had—but fear was another thing. Tenderness welled up in him. He hated Grayson for putting fear in her eyes.

"I'll walk you back."

"No." She shook her head. "It's not that."

"Then what is it?" he asked gently.

"You might get hurt."

He smiled, and something in his heart softened. She sassed him, could be a spitfire, until she thought he was in danger. "I promise I'll do my best to stay in one piece."

She shook her head, sending her hair in a swirl. Her blue eyes were enormous. It was all he could do not to pull her into his arms and hold her tight. Other than his mother, he couldn't think of a woman who'd ever been afraid for him. It was a potent feeling, one that touched him more deeply than their kisses the day before. He realized he was entering dangerous territory, but before he could pull back, emotionally and physically, she spoke again.

"You mentioned a policeman who stopped a bullet meant for a woman."

"So?" he asked carefully.

Her lower lip quivered. "Don't you see, I don't want that happening to you. True, you sometimes irritate me, and I wish you weren't here, but you are. If I suddenly leave now, and if Grayson's in the barn spying on us, he'll wonder why I've gone back to the house. We must not raise his suspicions. Look at you. It's a very warm day, and you're wearing a jacket. I'm in shorts and a top. Wouldn't you wonder about you if you were Grayson?"

She was watching him with an anxious appeal, and her tone of voice, the muscles working in her jaw, alerted him. He didn't know her well, but he did know that if she broke down and cried, he'd have his hands full. He was no good with crying women. The last time he'd consoled a sobbing woman, she'd formed the mistaken idea *he* came with the comfort. The time after that, when he hadn't offered a woman his shoulder, he'd felt like a louse afterward. He'd have to halt Polly's possible tears before they got started.

"Grayson's under constant surveillance," he said, trying to sound calm and logical. "I'd know if he was here."

"Could you guarantee me that? Can you?" she demanded.

He hesitated, then admitted, "Anything's possible."

"There, you see! You're ready to chance walking into the barn like a lamb to slaughter. What is it with you macho men? Don't you realize he could shoot you? You're unfair. You barge into my life, order me around, and now you could get killed on my property! Under my nose!"

He sighed. "I don't plan on getting killed."

She waved aside his objection. "It's ghastly. Think of the legacy you'd leave. Imagine how I would feel if I see your blood splattered on the ground. My ground. How do you think I'd feel if I had done nothing to prevent it?"

His hand came up to cup her cheek. "How would you feel?" he asked softly.

"I'd be a basket case. You'd ruin my life. Forever. I'd have unbearable nightmares. I probably wouldn't be able to hold on to my job, let alone finish my book. All because of your selfishness. Is that fair? Heck, I'm scared of thunder. When it gets too loud, I yank the covers over my head. I'm a certified coward. If I watch you walk to your death, I'd have to sell the family farm. The memories would be too painful. And then what would happen to Aunt Martha? Not to mention Horace and Cuddles. Well, Cuddles I could take with me, but a cow? Hardly."

Reid suspected she was winding up to some grand finale. He hated to interrupt, but he did. "Aren't you jumping to conclusions?"

She gripped his arm. "Please! We need to set the scene. Both of us."

He exhaled slowly. No point stopping her when

she was on a roll. He'd never seen a woman more hell-bent on having her say. "Okay. How should we go about it?"

Encouraged, she eased her death grip, but not by much. "Simple. We outsmart him."

"How?"

"Imagine you're writing a thriller or directing a movie."

Golden sunlight shimmered in her hair. Her eyes were fired with passion. Pity, he thought, it wasn't for him.

"At the rate we're going," he said, "I'm having a hard time remembering I'm a cop."

Missing the humor and intent on advancing her theory, she said, "If Grayson sees us out here, he's going to feel like a cornered cat. He'll probably be trigger-happy. We need to give him time for his adrenaline to slow down."

Reid saw she was dead serious. Her voice was trembling, her chin quivered, but she was bravely trying to cover her fears. He casually took her hand, pressing one finger over the pulse in her wrist. It was tripping like a jackhammer. He definitely needed to get her back to the house.

"If you don't turn around and walk back to the house," he said, "I'll get angry. Which do you want? Grayson's suspicion or my anger?"

She didn't hesitate a heartbeat. "I'll chance your

anger. I'm beginning to get used to your bite. Besides, I know how men think."

"So, you're a woman of the world?"

She blushed. "I wasn't born yesterday. Besides, writers are students of human nature. It's a trait creative people share. You said yourself that you can't guarantee Grayson isn't in the barn."

Seeing he had no choice but to play along, Reid said, "If he is in there, don't you think he's wondering what we're doing here?"

"All the more reason for us to fool him into thinking you're not a threat," she said in all earnestness.

"What do you propose we do?"

She gripped his arms. "The only thing we can do. Go into our act."

FIVE

"Act?" Reid asked, unsure of her meaning.

"Our kissing act."

He regarded her in amazement. She didn't particularly like him, but she was ready to kiss him on the gamble it would save his life.

"Stop wasting time," she said. "And for goodness' sake, stand sideways."

"Why?" he asked, his voice strangled.

"It's obvious. If you do, you'll be able to sneak a peek at the window in the loft, see if you can spot him. He'll be in the loft," she added confidently, "if he's in there."

"If Grayson is in there, wouldn't he sneak out the window on the far side of the loft?"

"Are you willing to chance it?"

"I see why you're a writer," he said, aware anew of her vulnerability. Her eyes beseeched him, and he knew if he refused her, he'd heighten her anxieties. She'd talked herself into this scenario. For her sake the least he could do was magnanimously play his part and kiss her.

The thought pleased him enormously. His mind raced ahead, triggering a response in his groin. "You have a wonderful imagination."

"Why, thank you," she said, momentarily distracted. "However, this isn't a plot."

"It should be." He cleared his throat, and with a clear conscience, pressed his advantage. "How do you propose we do this? Shall I put my arms around you first, or should you initiate the kiss?"

She frowned with concern. "Is it important?"

"I'm not sure," he said gravely. "They never trained me for this situation at the police academy."

"You're a cop. You're supposed to think on your feet."

He kept his expression as serious as he could. "Believe me, I am. All right. Your plan is best. Standing sideways allows me to whip my gun out faster and get a bead on him."

He saw the look of horror on her face and realized his error. "Don't think about it. Particularly now."

She gnawed her lower lip. "I can't help it. I know your job is dangerous. I mean, I know what I read, what I see on TV and in the movies. But with it happening here—"

"Polly."

She quieted, gazing up at him.

"Before we kiss," he said, "please remember I'm certain you're mistaken. I want you to relax. Block every man from your mind but me."

Including the jerk you have a date with tonight.

"When I release you, walk, don't run, back to the house. Lock the doors. Tell Fran to check upstairs. Then I want you to go into your bedroom and lie down on your bed. Don't leave until I come to get you."

She bobbed her head. Her lids fluttered closed. "You may kiss me now. Don't worry. This time I swear I'll cooperate. I'll do my absolute best."

A smile tugged at his lips. "Thank you. I swear I will too." His fingertips lightly caressed her cheek. He kissed her neck.

Her eyes snapped open. "Kiss my lips!" she hissed.

He cleared his throat to mask a choking sound. "I'm getting there."

"Grayson could shoot us before you do."

"I doubt it. Besides, if we're lovers, he'd expect this. We're playing a game of cat and mouse."

Reid ran his hands up the sides of her rib cage, his fingers straying to the undersides of her breasts. "If you're right, I want him to see us holding each other. Tightly. Melt against my chest."

She instantly plastered herself to him, starting a meltdown in Reid. Groaning inwardly, he rubbed his hands up and down her back.

"Yes, that's right, Polly. Now put your arms around my neck. Good. You're very receptive. I'm going to kiss your chin, then nibble a little on your ear. Feel free to do whatever you think will convince Grayson we're no threat to him."

She kissed his neck.

"My earlobe would be a good place too. Mmmm. That's wonderful. Do you like this?" he asked, returning the favor.

"Stop wasting time," she wailed, dropping her hands. "Remember Grayson's adrenaline."

Reid tilted up her chin and gazed into her sparkling eyes. Despite her apprehension and mounting fear, she insisted on putting herself in possible danger to help him. He kissed her temple.

"I'm thinking about your adrenaline." He brushed his mouth over hers. "Your adrenaline," he whispered, demonstrating his expertise in feather-light kisses on her lips. "I want your adrenaline soaring to the stratosphere. We only get one shot."

Polly shuddered. Dutifully, she let her hands creep up Reid's muscular chest. Considering that Grayson might be in the barn, she couldn't understand how Reid could be this cool, this calm. Did ice water run in all policemen's veins, or just in his?

"If it helps," she said, "pretend I'm Scarlett."

He cupped her face in his big hands. "Polly, please shut up so I can kiss you."

She flung her arms around his neck. Having decided that only her convincing performance could keep Grayson from suspecting Reid's true identity, she pressed her lips to his. His arms encircled her, and she slid her tongue into his mouth. A groan rumbled deep in his chest. Worried she'd gone too far, she tried retreating, but his tongue raked across her lips, her teeth, before tangling with hers.

Polly forgot about Grayson, forgot this kiss was supposed to be an act. She clung to Reid, joining wholeheartedly in his mind-blowing kiss. When she felt his hands on her derriere, she pressed even closer to him. He kissed her neck, her eyelids, her cheeks. She could feel him straining against her and dimly wondered if he was still acting, or if he, like she, had been caught up in the unexpected explosion of passion between them.

He broke the kiss, and his breathing was coming in short pants. "My God!"

"What?" she asked dazedly, stunned by her reaction to him.

Reid grazed her lower lip with his thumb. The first time he'd kissed her, he'd attributed his instant sexual reaction to his irritation at her goading him. He'd kissed her the second time because he couldn't believe the first time. Thanks to her generosity, she'd initiated this kiss. So what did he make of his reaction? Of how aroused he'd gotten?

"Damn," he said, awestruck, "you're either a hell of a convincing actress, or I'm so far gone I don't know it."

She frowned up at him, apparently still lost in

the heat generated by their kiss. Then she blinked and stepped back. "Oh." She glanced at the barn. "I changed my mind. If Grayson's up there, let him stay. Come back to the house with me. Don't be a dead hero."

The radio clicked off. Silence. Then they heard a series of loud, long moos. Horace.

She sighed with relief. "If anyone were there with him, Horace wouldn't moo. She's finicky. You must have been right. I must have set the timer wrong."

She looked so happy, he resisted the urge to pull her into his arms and kiss her again. He had to play the scene out. "I'll check. Go back to the house. I'll come for you when it's safe."

"Be careful," she said, her eyes going soft and luminous. "It still might be a trick."

He gave her a brief hug. If he didn't get hold of his emotions, he told himself, he'd be in danger of becoming as mushy as Ashley Wilkes. "You're one terrific partner. Now go on, I'll be fine."

The barn, a traditionally designed building with grayed boards, had a set of wide, high doors at either end. Before entering, he checked the outer perimeter and found it safe. Inside, the barn smelled of leather, wood, hay, and animal. Shafts of light filtered through the slats and the open door. Dust motes danced in the air.

Horace, who Polly claimed acted finicky around strangers, greeted him with brown-eyed curiosity, several swishes of her tail, and a mooed hello. Then she tried to lick his face.

"Stop it! I'll kiss your mistress anytime, but not you."

So much for Horace acting nasty toward strangers, he thought. Or else the cow had seen them kissing by peering out the window near Axl Rose's poster, and figured if he was good enough for Polly, he couldn't be bad. His theory couldn't be nuttier than a cow being a fan of Axl Rose.

Walking to the center of the barn, he looked around. It could best be described as the neatest mess he'd ever seen. Old and rusted machinery was shoved up against one wall. On another hung various large and small gardening tools. Near a metal cabinet was a lawn mower, plus bags of fertilizer, bundles of hay, and an aluminum ladder. Close by the door leading to the pasture, he spotted a pile of roofing shingles and a tarpaulin.

His downstairs inspection over, he climbed up to the hayloft. Remaining on the top step, he let his gaze sweep the interior. Finding it empty, he stepped back down to the main floor. Remembering that Polly had been about to take Horace to the pasture, he led the cow outside. After checking the barn once more, he sat down on a bale of hay and dropped his head in his hands.

He'd never been in a crazier situation. He started to chuckle, but remorse abruptly cut off his laughter.

One fact was irrefutable. Polly had set aside her fears to save him. The more time he spent with her, the more he appreciated her rare and special qualities. He strode from the barn, his pace quick, eager to see her face when he told her the good news.

"False alarm," he shouted as he entered the house.

Polly flew downstairs, her eyes shining with joyous relief. The brilliant smile on her face filled him with delight. Reid had never seen anyone glow with such happiness. Without thinking, he picked her up and twirled her around. Her hair brushed his cheeks. Then, realizing he was holding her longer than the situation warranted, he put her down.

"Thank you for caring," he said quietly.

"You're welcome," she said, just as quietly.

Fran entered the room. "You two look happy. I take it Grayson's not in the barn. I didn't think he was."

Reid gave her a stern look. "Polly was right to warn me to take precautions."

Fran's eyebrows rose at her partner's serious retort, but she only said that she was off on their other case. "Don't plan on me for supper," she added. "And Reid, I'll need to borrow your car, please. My battery died."

He handed her his car keys. "Bring a new battery back with you. I'll install it."

As soon as Fran left, Reid hugged Polly again. "You were wonderful."

Their gazes met and held. Reid was acutely aware that they were alone for the rest of the day, and perhaps part of the night too. He'd never before gotten involved with a woman who was part of a case he was working on, yet Polly was a nearly irresistible temptation. Against his will, his gaze drifted to her breasts. He wanted to taste her there too. Fortunately, she spoke, forcing his mind away from her delectable body and back to his job.

"Don't you worry about putting your life in danger?"

He took a step back from her, attempting to put some professional distance between them. "Every sensible law-enforcement officer worries, but you can't let it stop you. When and if I leave the force, I'll become a prosecutor, help put the bad guys behind bars for a long time instead of merely arresting them.

"Polly, we didn't finish talking about your date tonight. I'd appreciate it if you would break it. It could blow my cover." He cleared his throat. "To make up for it, I could take you out instead. Just to dinner. Since Fran won't be here."

Polly studied his disconcerted expression with great interest. The cool, always-in-control Detective Reid Cameron seemed unusually ill at ease. Was he asking her out to dinner as a way of apologizing for the havoc he was wreaking in her life—or were his reasons more personal? And which was safer for her?

"All right," she said, trying to banish from her

mind the delightful image of her and Reid dancing to a romantic melody. She took several steps away from him. "Now, if you'll excuse me, I'm going to get some writing done."

She went into her pine-paneled den, but if she thought she'd be free of Reid with a door between them, she was wrong. He filled her thoughts. At first she had resented him. Now she viewed him in a new light. He hadn't taken advantage of her fears out by the barn. Though he'd tried to convince her that Grayson wasn't nearby, he'd treated her with kindness and consideration, even going along with her crazy plan. Going along with it? He'd put one hundred percent effort into it. Her face heated as she remembered their passionate embrace, the way their bodies had almost gone up in flames as they'd pressed close to each other.

Turning abruptly to her computer, she tried to attribute her heightened awareness of him to the drama his presence had brought into her life. Her orderly existence lacked the elements of danger that attracted a man like Reid to the police. By contrast, teaching kindergarten must seem drab to him. She was better off in her little world, where she knew the schedule, took pleasure from her teaching and writing. When she wanted electrifying, nerve-shattering experiences, she found them in the theater, movies, and books.

She switched on the computer and brought up the chapter she was working on. As she struggled for an hour, her mind kept wandering to Reid. Did he think she was rude, ignoring him like this? Or, even worse, did he think she was afraid of him?

At best her writing efforts were sluggish. She didn't need an editor to tell her the love scene lacked fire. Pushing her chair back, she rose and walked around the room. She did stretching exercises. Hearing Cuddles scratching at the door, she let him in. He flopped down in his usual position on a square of shag carpeting she'd placed for him near her chair.

She thought about making herself a cup of coffee, but discarded the idea. Sitting down at the computer again, she told herself writing was 90 percent perspiration and 10 percent inspiration.

Closing her eyes, she pictured her lovers. In her mind's eye she saw the tall, dark-haired hero's smile, as intimate as a kiss. Much the same as the smile Reid had given her when he'd swung her around. Then he had grinned broadly. She had, too, for she'd felt grateful he hadn't met with harm. She thought again of how Reid had treated her concerns with respect, while tempering her worries.

Her hero would show her heroine similar consideration. Their eyes would share a special secret, triggered by emotions too powerful for her heroine to deal with in this one scene. Her heroine reacted purely on the shock of discovery, on the sensual pull of the hero's potent presence, the private message his body communicated to hers. Polly knew her heroine's emotions, for like the fictional woman, she'd experienced firsthand the magnificence of a man. Her heroine would respond to the hero with a sense of urgency, brought about as the hero's hands and kisses awakened each sensory nerve ending.

Polly felt herself transported. As she gave her heroine desires she couldn't deny, evocative words and images flowed from Polly's brain. Pages filled the screen as the love scene vibrated with emotion. When she finished, she read what she'd written.

She paled. She hadn't written fiction. She'd chronicled her turbulent fears, which had led to her kissing Reid, and had ended the scene with the heroine in an emotional turmoil, knowing her life would never again be the same.

Polly copied the chapter onto another disk and switched off the computer. "Girl, you're nuts," she muttered aloud. "You're foolishly sentimental and grossly dramatic."

It was time for her to put Reid's mission in its proper perspective. If she could assist him to leave more quickly, she would. Her decision made, she went in search of him. She wanted to know more about Reid. If Grayson posed a threat to her, he posed a greater threat to Reid. A shiver ran through her. She could shut off her story a lot more easily than she could control the turbulent events in her real life.

❧ ———————— ❧

Reid heard Polly moving around in the den and resisted the desire to storm her hallowed sanctuary and confess he was as stunned as she. Whenever he got near her, sparks flew. He couldn't deny the way she made him feel, or his surprise at how quickly his attraction to her was growing. But what could he do about it?

He strolled into the bright kitchen, deliciously scented with potpourri and made cheerful by the little touches that attested to Polly's home-loving care. He took a can of soda from the refrigerator and popped the lid. As he sipped the soda, he admired the rough-hewn elm kitchen table, on which she'd placed a blue earthenware vase filled with a bouquet of spring flowers. He sat on the cushioned window bench, which displayed Polly's needlework talent. Gazing out the window, he saw a line of darkening gray clouds in the east shrouding the sky. It was beginning to mask the mountain peaks.

Finished with his soda, he rinsed and tossed the empty can into the recycling pail, then wandered into the living room. Here the furniture consisted of oak and mahogany pieces, comfortable couches, chairs, and a recliner. An upright Baldwin piano stood against one wall. On the occasional tables and the fireplace mantle were family pictures.

He peered at them. The first was of a crying Polly. She looked about two and was sitting on Santa Claus's lap. Her hair was coming loose from her pigtails, her knees sported Band-Aids, and she'd clenched her little hands into fists.

He shook his head, smiling. "Santa, she's still clenching her fists."

Another picture had him laughing aloud. Taken when she was about six years old, wearing pigtails that defied their clasps, the imp was missing her two front teeth. She was standing in front of her parents, sporting a shiner on her right eye, and grinning into the camera.

There were a few snapshots of her father and mother, several others that obviously captured special celebrations. A more serious photograph showed Polly in cap and gown, holding her high school diploma, her parents flanking her. Too bad her parents weren't alive to see their lovely daughter now.

Polly stood in the doorway, taking a moment to study Reid. He exuded a sense of raw power, yet with lithe grace. He combined authority and sexuality. He had eyes like a midnight avenger. A penetrating gaze capable, she suspected, of seeing beyond the obvious, to the soul.

As if sensing her presence, he turned. He gave her a long, heated look, then smiled.

Wow! she thought. His smile could kindle a fire. It lit a warmth throughout her body that flashed to a fiery heat as she remembered his arms crushing her, his lips covering hers.

"All finished?" he asked.

"Yes. I'm sorry if it seemed I was running out on you before. I wanted to get a few pages done. About tonight, Reid . . . My aunt will be coming over later this afternoon, and since I haven't seen her for a couple of days, I'd like to ask her to stay for dinner. We can go out after she leaves, maybe to a movie. Do you think Fran will be back by then? We could ask her to go with us."

"I don't need a chaperon." His keen look asked the silent question *Do you?*

"I didn't mean that you do," she said, marveling at his uncanny ability to read her mind.

"Yes, you did. Polly, be honest with yourself. Whatever is happening with us has you as flabbergasted as it has me. You're as amazed as I am."

Rather than answer, she led him out onto the screened-in porch that ran the length of one side of the house. The back wall was painted sunny yellow, with white trompe-l'oeil trellises on it. Like the front veranda, the porch had wicker furniture, including a graceful Victorian rocking chair.

"This room gets the afternoon sun," she said. "My mother dubbed it our solarium. She said it sounded grand."

"It's better than grand," Reid said, feeling an immediate affinity for the spacious enclosure. "For all its size, it's cozy. Makes me yearn to put my feet up on a footstool, lean back in one of these chairs, and enjoy the scenery."

"Fran made a similar comment. She said it's a far cry from city noise. My parents installed storm windows and heat for use year-round. The front porch gets the morning sun. Between the two, I watch both sunrise and sunset."

"What's your favorite time of day?"

"Sunset. There's a sighing softness to it, like the closing pages of a good book. Everything is tinged with feeling. The mountains glow."

"Like your hair," he said. It rested on her shoulders, curling upward like fingers reaching toward the light. Resisting the urge to touch that hair, he bent down to examine the Victorian rocker, whose reeds showed signs of distress. "Sun damages wicker. The rays dry the reeds. They get brittle as a result."

"Where did you learn about wicker?"

"Mostly from my mother. She repairs wicker furniture. After my dad died, she turned her hobby into a business. I often help her ready chairs for restoring, checking and redrilling existing holes for her to weave and seamlessly blend new reeds with the old. Tension and moisture are critical for weaving wicker."

"You surprise me."

He looked up at her. "Why? Didn't you think cops have private lives?"

"Sorry. I didn't mean to pry into your affairs."

He squeezed her hand. "You're not. It's okay. I noticed it's clouding up. As long as we have time before your aunt comes, how about if I set some of those loose shingles inside the barn on the roof?"

They were standing close to each other. Awareness flowed through him. Her scent tantalized him. She started to lean toward him, then she pulled back. "Polly, I . . ."

"Don't," she pleaded. "Nothing is happening to us. I won't allow it. Maybe going out tonight isn't a good idea."

"Polly, Fran isn't coming back until very late. We're alone, whether we go out or stay here. And personally, I'd much rather go dancing with you than sit in a dark movie theater watching some summertime action-adventure film."

His gaze dropped to her hands. They were clenched so tightly, her knuckles were turning white. "Just forget it," he said. Muttering a soft oath, he shoved open the porch door and walked away.

At the barn, he lugged the ladder outside, set it up, then went back in for the shingles. He began carrying them up to the roof, making several trips.

When he descended for his last batch of shingles, he saw Polly standing at the foot of the ladder. "What are you doing here?"

"Reid, this is silly. I got to thinking about the diamonds."

He drew his arm across his forehead, wiping away the sweat. "What about them?"

"If you find them, I think you should leave them alone. Don't switch them with cubic zirconiums. How can you arrest him for carrying fake diamonds? The most you can arrest him for is trespassing."

"I can arrest him for a string of burglaries, selling drugs, and more. Including prostitution."

"You never told me!" she said, her voice rising.

He pursed his lips. "I wasn't aware I had to. The only order of yours I'm aware of is not to make love to you." If she wanted to lie to herself, fine. He wasn't going to. He'd felt her passion. She'd felt his. "Do you want the reward money or not?"

"Of course I do. I just don't think you should waste time hunting for the jewels."

"If I know where he's stashed them, it makes my job easier. I'll know where he's headed. It eliminates the guesswork."

That seemed to satisfy her, but then she stepped up onto the ladder.

"Where do you think you're going?" he asked.

"With you. I want to help."

"Do me a big favor, don't."

"Don't be silly. Two of us will work faster. I'll hand you shingles. Afterward, I'll help you search."

"Go away. Polly. In case you haven't noticed, when we're near each other, fireworks start. I don't need distraction."

"I'll also be your lookout."

"I told you Grayson won't be here before Monday or Tuesday."

"You also told me the police bugged his car. Can you guarantee he won't change automobiles? Can you?"

Reid gave up. He couldn't guarantee squat. Including what was happening to him. The longer he remained with her, the more he wanted to make love to her. He nearly lost his balance thinking of what he'd like to do with her in the hayloft.

It wasn't easy for him to put down the temporary cover without the aid of the wooden crossbeams roofers use for footrests, but he managed.

"Have you done this before too?" Polly asked as she handed him several more shingles.

He wiped his face on his sleeve. "No. I watch *This Old House* on TV. One of the programs was devoted to putting down a new roof. This is the wrong way, but it won't hurt what the roofer will do later. I'm not gluing or nailing."

He looked over his job. "Without supports, that's as high as I can go."

They climbed down. He put the ladder back where he'd found it, then they both washed their hands at the sink inside the barn.

"Now what?" Polly asked.

"I'm going diamond hunting. You do what you want."

"Reid, please."

"Don't 'Reid, please' me. I'm in a lousy mood. I'll get over it."

Her gaze bounced nervously from him to the loft. "I insist."

"Suit yourself."

"What makes you think the diamonds are up there?"

"It's a hunch. I have to start someplace. Put yourself in Grayson's head. He doesn't know how often you move things around, but he grew up on a farm. He knows Horace grazes in the field. Her added feed is down here, plus the hay you've got stacked down here is enough to last several weeks or a month."

Polly stared at him with respect. As well as being tall and handsome and wonderfully fit, with the most expressive eyes, he was good at his job.

The hayloft occupied a space approximately half the size of the barn. The afternoon heat coupled with the sun that streamed in through the window made the loft a good eight degrees warmer than the barn below. Reid opened the window. From that vantage point, he had a clear view of the house.

He extended his hand to Polly. "Take a look at the angle."

She joined him at the window. For her to see out, he stepped behind her. Polly stared out the window, but his presence was too distracting. Her inner temperature soared even higher than the loft's, and arousal raced through her veins. Turning her head, she swallowed when she found him looking at her lips. "What should I be seeing?"

"Your bedroom window. When Grayson comes, don't go in there. If he has a high-powered rifle, he'll have a clear shot."

"Oh, dear," she murmured.

He reached into his pocket and withdrew a bracelet with a colorful stone in its center. "Wear this, starting Monday. In an emergency depress the stone. It's a transmitter. Either Fran or I will respond."

Polly could feel the tension in her neck. "You have all the modern trinkets."

"This is so I can keep you safe."

She bobbed her head. "You want Grayson for more than stealing jewels, selling drugs, and dealing in prostitution, don't you?"

He drew a harsh breath. "Yes. We think he's connected to a murder. Would you rather I pretend there's no danger, like I'm pretending I don't want you in my arms now?"

She leaned back against his chest. He wrapped his arms around her. "I think," she whispered, an involuntary shiver running through her, "that I'm very glad you're here."

For several moments they stood in silence, then she whispered his name.

"Mmmm?"

"This isn't a bit like one of my romance plots."

He pressed his lips to the sensitive spot behind her ear. "Turn it into one after I leave. By then you'll know the outcome of your story."

That was fine for her heroine, she thought, but what about her?

SIX

With effort Polly stepped out of Reid's embrace and turned her mind back to the reason for Reid being there. "If Grayson isn't due until Monday, technically you could go home and come back Sunday night, couldn't you?"

He gazed into her eyes. "Wasn't it you who told me I can't give you guarantees?"

"Yes, but you seem sure about his movements. Why not take a break, send another trooper, then return?"

He reached out and brushed one hand down her hair. "I'm on assignment. Are you ready to go diamond hunting and cash in on your reward?"

"What about your share?"

"There is no share. This is part of my job."

They worked as a team. Marking off the loft in thirds, Reid raked the hay aside. Laboriously they sifted through hundreds of pieces of straw. Doing only one section took over an hour.

Her back aching, Polly stood to arch it, then pointed to a section of the hay, saying, "I'm going to hunt through this area alone. Maybe it will go faster."

He didn't argue with her. She dropped to her knees and began searching. "Do you know if the diamonds are set or loose?" she asked.

"Both, according to the jeweler's manifest."

She nodded. They worked for another half hour but didn't find anything. As she started to search through another section, Reid happened to glance up. He froze when he spotted the thin, nearly invisible wire. It could only mean one thing. Grayson had rigged a charge! The selfish bastard must have figured if he couldn't have the jewels, no one could, even if it meant maiming or killing innocent people.

"Polly." Reid's voice was low, assertive. Any sudden move on her part could shift the straw around the base of the charge and trigger the mechanism.

She looked up. Bits of straw clung to her hair. "It's futile, isn't it?"

"I think we should quit for today. Polly, I'm about to tell you what to do. Please don't ask questions. Do exactly as I ask."

She heard the warning in his voice, saw his taut expression. "May I move my head?" she asked, her voice as tense as his face.

"Yes, but first put the straw in your hand down. Don't stand. Stay on your knees. I'm coming over to get you."

Her eyes went wide. "What is it?"

"There's a colorless wire to your right, about five inches from you. It resembles fishing line. I don't trust what it's connected to. I don't want to take any chances. It's probably nothing, but just to make sure, please, don't move."

Fear clogged her throat. "It's a bomb, isn't it?"

"I won't lie to you. I'm not certain."

She clenched her teeth. "It is a bomb, isn't it?"

"If it is, it's a crude one. I'll dismantle it."

"No. Let's get out of here." Her words were barely audible. Just yesterday morning her biggest worry was writing a love scene. Compared to the terrifying possibility that the slightest wrong move could set off a charge, her plot problem dwindled to nothing. Bile reached her throat. She bit down hard on her lip and tasted blood.

She concentrated on Reid's voice encouraging her. He said it was probably a groundless worry, she was doing fine. He was proud of her, he said as he inched his way toward her, carefully moving aside hay.

He positioned himself at her back, placing his hands on her waist. Nothing in the world had ever felt as welcome as his strong hands, or his lips near her ear, murmuring how proud he was of her for following his instructions. She knew she was a basket case, but he never raised his voice.

"I'm going to slide you away," he said. "This way it displaces less hay. You'll be on your knees, sweetheart, but I can't help that."

She bobbed her head as his endearment echoed in her mind. Her insides were liquid. Trusting him implicitly, she did as he asked, letting herself go limp as he drew her backward.

"Stay with me, sweetheart, you're doing fine. Only a few more inches, then we'll rest a second before standing."

When they reached the edge of the loft, he helped her stand, then made sure she climbed safely down the ladder. He led her quickly outside, wrapped one arm around her quaking shoulders, and walked her to the house. "Go inside. I'll be right there."

"Where are you going?"

"To diffuse the mechanism."

"Don't!" she pleaded, flinging her arms around his neck. "Let the old barn blow up. Horace is outside. A pile of wood is replaceable. You're not."

He cupped her cheek, his heart reaching out to her. "Polly," he replied, his voice strangely husky to his own ears, "I was sent here to do a job. Please don't interfere. I know what I'm doing."

"Can you guarantee that?" she demanded, the words exploding from her as she stared at him with terror-stricken eyes. "If you destroy the bomb, Grayson will know, so what have you gained?"

"Your safety, which is as important to me as mine is to yours. Do you think I'd let you run a risk if I can help it? I can rig it so it looks as if it wasn't touched. Anyway, Horace needs her stall."

"My neighbor can take her."

"It will ruin my cover. Please, I know what I'm doing."

"I hate Grayson! He's not worth your getting killed."

"I can't stand here arguing." His arm slid around her waist. "I'd rather kiss you than talk anyway."

She stamped her foot. "Sex! At a time like this, you think of sex?"

He chuckled. "Only a kiss. We'll take care of the rest later."

Clenching her fist, she looked into his drugging dark eyes and rated her chances of knocking him out cold. In a flash she understood why he wanted to kiss her.

"I'm on to you, Cameron. You think you can divert my attention. It won't work. If you kiss me now, I'll bite off your tongue. You're a damned fool!"

A flash of respect came into his eyes, and she knew she had guessed his intentions. He wanted her to feed on her anger, preferring it over her fears for his safety.

She turned on her heel, her feet crunching the ground. Inside the house she picked up Cuddles, ran upstairs to her room, and flung herself on the bed.

"God," she prayed. "Keep him in one piece. Please."

Trying to console herself that Reid knew what he was doing didn't help. She gazed around her dream bedroom, decorated in white. She'd let her imagination and her talented fingers transform it into an intimate boudoir.

It had a canopied bed, with a white rosette-embroidered Indian cotton bedspread, and pillowcases ruffled in layers of lace.

How could this be? How could she idly do nothing? Wait to possibly hear a deadly explosion? If she phoned the police, they couldn't arrive in time to help.

She willed herself to think of anything but Reid searching through shifting straw for a bomb that might explode before he rendered it harmless.

She started getting off the bed to go to him, then sagged against the pillow. He'd asked—correction, he'd ordered—her to wait. If she disturbed him, she could break his concentration, possibly cause him harm. Her stomach churning with apprehension, she decided she'd give him a few more minutes. In the meantime she curled her knees to her chest, closed her eyes, and prayed for his safety.

That was consoling for only a couple of minutes. Fretting, she glanced at the clock on the dresser. What was taking him this long? Maybe the charge had gone off and his body had muffled its sound? Maybe he wished she could hear him?

Maybe she was driving herself batty?

For the next ten minutes she asked herself unanswerable questions, most of them foolish, but all of them focused on Reid's safety. An ache of sadness gripped her. Scalding hot tears streamed from her eyes. So awful was the thought of Reid wounded or worse, she had to forcibly wipe it from her mind.

Finally she couldn't stand it any longer. Rolling off the bed, she inched to the window that looked out on the barn, rising on her knees to peek outside. She strained her eyes but saw nothing unusual. If Reid were in danger, he was in it alone. He and Grayson. Dammit, she felt helpless. She hated that feeling.

Despite his attempts to play it down with Polly, Reid faced an extremely dangerous situation. One false move would set off the charge and blow him to kingdom come. His thigh ached, but he stayed rigidly still as he took a few minutes to mentally review the steps he had to follow. Saying a quick prayer, he began. He directed his fingers to move slowly, carefully, and with perspiration beading on his face, he dismantled the timing mechanism.

He sat back on his haunches, waiting for his breath to even out. He held his hands in front of him. Steady before, they now shook. Wiping his face, he dropped his head forward and rolled his shoulders to relieve the kink in his neck.

In minutes he located two soft bags stuffed with loose and mounted diamonds: brooches, earrings, necklaces, and rings. As he held a necklace up to the light, the gems blazed with fire. Grayson knew what to steal. Polly's reward should be substantial. Setting the bags aside, he fixed the wiring to make it appear as if it hadn't been touched. As he rose from his crouched position, he caught sight of a diamond ring on the floor partially hidden by straw. Grayson must have dropped it.

Reid pocketed the ring, grabbed the bags, and descended the ladder. For the second time in less than a year he'd been lucky to stay alive. As he headed for the house, he wondered what sort of mood Polly was in.

He'd hoped to alleviate her fears but knew he'd failed. Her eyes had told him all he needed to know. She had been deeply worried, and the thought of her caring what happened to him appealed to him.

Inside the house he found her curled up on her bed in a fetal position, her dog sleeping beside her. Her hair hid her face, and one fist was slowly beating the bedspread.

"It's okay," he said, putting his hand on her shoulder and turning her around. He tried to smile at her, but what he saw in her wounded blue eyes nearly sent him to his knees with regret for what she'd been put through that day.

He sat down beside her and laid his hand against her cheek. "It's over," he said as tenderly as he could.

Her gaze swiftly covered his body from head to toe, looking for signs he'd been hurt. Her hands slid up his chest to his shoulders. "You okay?"

"Yes." He framed her face, his thumbs wiping away her tears. "Honey, I'm sorry. Grayson's an idiot. He didn't rig a smart charge. It was a piece of cake to dismantle. And look."

He grinned with triumph as he held up the bags of jewels. "You're going to get a hefty reward."

When Polly saw his delighted expression, as if he'd come from a walk in the park, while she'd nearly died with fright, all her emotions exploded into anger.

"How dare you pacify me with this? Do you know how worried I was? Do you know what you put me through? Then you come here with this . . . stuff! Go away," she spat contemptuously, her eyes fiercely accusing as she dismissed a fortune in diamonds.

Reid put the bags on the bed, unperturbed by her outburst. He understood that her concern for him was behind her release of tension. And he was even sorrier he hadn't been able to give her guarantees. Though he had expert training, accidents happened in the best of circumstances. She'd gotten the scare of her life. With good cause. The fear she'd kept inside her while wondering if he'd be injured or killed had terrified her. She'd said she was afraid of thunder.

He wrapped his arms around her and pulled her tightly to his chest. "It's okay," he murmured, stroking her hair.

Her tears wet his shirt. "Go away. I don't want anything to do with you. Play cops and robbers somewhere else. I wish I'd never met you. You took over my life."

"Have I?" he asked, feeling absurdly happy that she cared enough to cry over him.

"Yes. From the minute we met. I don't like it! I don't know how you do it, Reid. How do you stay so calm?" Her voice rose with accusation. "It's a piece of cake to you. That's what you said. Your typical day's work."

"No, I promise you I don't do this every day."

"No wonder there's such a high divorce rate among cops."

He was silent for a long moment, then said, "Maybe it's better if you go away until this is over."

She shook her head, drawing in a ragged breath. "I can't. There's Martha. She's an old lady."

"Why should it matter? Show me how to milk Horace, and take Martha away with you. I'll let you know when to return."

"We've been through this. Martha has a doctor's appointment Tuesday. She's secure in knowing she keeps her visits. I'm staying," she said belligerently.

Sighing, he rose to bring her some tissues. She blew her nose.

"Feel better now?" he asked gruffly.

She pushed back her hair. "No. I won't feel better until Grayson's locked up. That tawdry rat took away my most precious possession. My peace of mind." She plucked at the bedspread, sliding him a sidelong glance. "Thanks for saving my life." She sounded so reluctant, he laughed.

"You're welcome. I was glad to do it."

She stared moodily at the canopy above her bed. "I'm sorry I yelled. I shouldn't take my anger at Grayson out on you. And I'm sure Horace thanks you too."

Relief and amusement rushed through him. What a woman! She insisted on acting as his lookout on the roof, helped him hunt for the diamonds, demanded he let the barn blow up rather than risk getting hurt. Bright color dotted her flushed face. Her thick hair tumbled about her shoulders. She shifted her gaze, facing him with smoldering eyes.

"Keep looking at me like that," he said huskily, "I'll forgive you anything."

"Looking at you how?"

"Like a woman who can't decide if she wants to throttle me or make love to me. You've done the first. How about if we—"

"That's another thing," Polly interrupted before he could finish. He was lethal, worse than the dynamite charge he'd dismantled. He was a walking, talking, broad-shouldered, narrow-hipped, devilish sex bomb, who looked better in jeans than any man had a right to look! "This constant kissing," she went on, "must stop. It's disconcerting."

"Disconcerting? That's what you call what we're feeling? I've got a better name for it. And as I recall, you started it the last time, I didn't."

They exchanged smiles. Whom were they kidding?

"You're impossible. I'm glad you're safe, you big lug."

They heard the front door open and a birdlike voice call out, "Hellooo. Polly, are you upstairs?"

Reid groaned. "Martha?"

Polly rolled off the bed and stood. She glimpsed herself in the mirror. "I look a fright. My eyes are puffy. Martha must not see me this way."

Calling down to her aunt that she'd be right there, she dashed into the bathroom and washed her face. She applied fresh makeup, stepping aside for Reid to use the sink. He washed his own face and combed his hair.

She picked up her hairbrush, then caught him studying her in the mirror. He gave her an engaging smile, one packed with lazy sensuality.

"What?" she asked.

"Have you noticed whenever we're together, sparks fly."

Their gazes clinging, he took the hairbrush from her hand and drew it through her hair. Sparks of static electricity crackled in the air. He dipped his head and kissed her neck. His breath sent shivers down her spine.

"Electricity," he murmured. "We make our own."

"Martha's waiting," she said, her voice a low whisper.

"Too bad."

When she was almost out the door, he caught her wrist. In the flash of a second she was in his arms.

"Don't stop me," he said. "I've got a good reason. I'm preparing us for our act."

Before she could protest, his mouth captured hers, moving insistently over her lips. He boldly pressed his hips forward. One hand sank into her hair, holding her head still.

The kiss exploded into a fiercely wild mating, partly as a result of the dreadful fears she'd experienced and partly because she was unable to resist him. When he lifted his head, he looked at her with stormy passion darkening his eyes, murmured her name, then kissed her again.

A fire raged inside Reid. This one woman was capable of making him care deeply, while sending his blood to a boiling point. He released her and forced himself to sound casual as he said, "You've got that dewy radiant look. Remember, sweetheart, we're supposed to be madly in love."

She only stared at him dazedly, and he smiled as he steered her out of the bathroom and down the stairs.

Aunt Martha reminded Reid of a tiny general in a polka-dot red dress. She had a cap of blond curls, twin dimples, lively deep blue eyes, and a sprightly bounce to her walk. She was Polly's father's older sister by twelve years.

"I never guessed," she exclaimed, after she was introduced to Reid. "Imagine hiding this gorgeous man. I forgive you."

Polly exchanged helpless looks with Reid.

"I wasn't hiding him, Aunt Martha. We . . . we knew each other a long time ago."

Martha went on for her. "You broke up but you found each other again. It's in the timing. You weren't ready before. Now you are. I can see it in your eyes."

"It's wonderful, isn't it?" Reid said. "She's got that dewy radiance love brings out."

Martha nodded. Polly rolled her eyes. Reid winked at her.

"When did you know Reid was the man for you?" Martha asked.

Polly didn't answer, and Reid finally said, "She's still getting over the shock. We're engaged." He pulled the diamond ring from his pocket and snatched her left hand.

Polly gasped as he slipped the ring on her finger.

Martha beamed. "Oh, how wonderful. Since you're getting married, it's okay that you're staying here. Otherwise, it wouldn't be right. I like a take-charge man. Show me your ring, dear."

Polly's hand was still captured in Reid's, so he thrust it toward Martha for inspection. The round solitaire was set in platinum. Diamond baguettes were set on either side of the stone, which had to be at least three carats. Amazingly the ring fit perfectly.

Engaged! Polly thought. To a man she'd known little more than a day. Wearing a stolen ring—hot ice—as the promise of his sham affections. A daredevil lunatic who disarmed bombs. A lawman who kissed like a dream and made her sizzle. A slippery, sexy eel who would never be like Ashley Wilkes in a million years!

"To think," her aunt gushed, "I'm witnessing a momentous occasion."

"I'd say we all are," Reid said dryly.

Martha nudged him. "Aren't you going to kiss her?"

He chuckled. "Aunt Martha, you read my mind."

He took a stunned Polly in his arms and kissed her for Martha's benefit. When he lifted his head, she kept her back to Martha and hissed, "Stop this farce!"

His lips brushed her cheek. "Shut up, darling," he whispered. "It was your idea to let Martha stay. You're not acting like a woman in love, though, and you might have raised her suspicions. I couldn't have that."

He turned to Martha. "Look at her, Aunt Martha. May I call you Aunt Martha?"

"Please do. You're family now. You were saying?"

"Polly has a dewy radiance in her eyes."

Martha peered at her niece. "I see what you mean."

Polly suddenly realized that Reid was crazy like a fox. He had Martha eating from his hand, approving of his sleeping in her house.

"When is the wedding?" Martha asked.

Polly coughed. "We haven't set the date."

Martha put on her glasses. "Let me have your hand, Reid. I want to see what your palm says."

She studied his palm for a few minutes, then smiled with delight as she wiggled his pinkie finger. "It's here. One marriage. That's good. I see twins. Boys, I think. Then a boy and a girl. Polly, give my your hand."

While Reid sat with his mouth open, Polly smirked at him. Martha bent Polly's pinkie finger, examining a crease, then read her palm.

"Yes!" she cried. "This confirms it. You and Reid are going to have four children." Polly protested, but Martha insisted she was right.

"So," Martha said to Reid, "when you came back, you knew immediately. Just like that, you both knew, didn't you? You couldn't deny your feelings. Oh, this is too astounding for words." Martha gave him a coy look. "When did you know you were in love with Polly?"

"Umm, the first time we kissed. Wasn't it then, darling?"

"I wouldn't know," she replied tightly.

"Yes, I would say then. If not the first time, the second time. It hit me between the eyes. It gets better and better. I shouldn't be telling you this—"

Martha inched her chair closer. He gave her a roguish grin. "I don't mind telling you, she's quite a woman. I love holding her."

"Reid."

"Oh, shush, Polly," Martha said. "I want to hear this. Go make dinner. Reid and I want to get to know each other. It takes a real he-man to state his feelings. Too many men hide behind them, as if they're ashamed of having them."

"Like that wimp Ashley Wilkes," Reid said.

"You're absolutely right!" Martha exclaimed.

"Reid."

"Hush, Polly," Martha said. "You'd think you were as old as I am. People think," she added to Reid, "that when you reach your late seventies, you're over the hill. Go on, Reid."

With an ease Polly hadn't known was possible, he reconstructed their fantasy love affair. He supplied details, hinted of wonderful things they had supposedly done together in the past. Her knees grew weak. His imagination equaled, maybe even surpassed, hers. She dropped into a chair to listen to his pack of lies, knowing that if he put them on paper, he'd have a sizzling romance novel.

But what really amazed her was her aunt's reaction. She clearly was eating it up. Every once in a while Martha's blue-veined hands would fly to her mouth. A faraway look would come into her eyes, as if she were reliving a love affair herself. When she did, Reid slowed the story, giving her time to savor her memories. Other times, she giggled and bounced on her chair, clapping her little hands in glee.

Unable to stop him, Polly gave up trying and started dinner. She took a package of chopped meat from the refrigerator, slit the plastic wrapping, and dumped the contents into a plastic bowl with such force, the bowl bounced on the counter. She hacked an onion with a butcher knife and added more parsley than she normally would. With Reid adding relish to his recital, she slapped and formed hamburgers and thought about hurling one at his head.

While he fed Martha more whoppers, Polly washed and snapped string beans, then set them to cook in a pot of water where she normally steamed her vegetables. She tore lettuce leaves and sliced tomatoes, then set them on a plate, which she nearly dropped as she carried it to the table.

"What do you do?" Martha asked Reid as Polly set the plate down.

"He's an attorney," Polly answered quickly.

Martha's eyes glowed, and her dainty rosebud mouth formed a little O. "Why that's wonderful. Simply wonderful. And so practical. We'll have a teacher and a lawyer in the family. I want to make an appointment to update my will."

She giggled. "Polly knows I adore children. You do want them, don't you, dears?"

Torn between wanting to strangle Reid and not cause her aunt disappointment, Polly valiantly responded in a way calculated not to dim her aunt's enthusiasm.

"Of course. Maybe not so soon, though."

"I could be wrong about the exact timing," Martha said, "although I think it will be ten months after the wedding." She touched Reid's hand. "It's only natural that you and Polly want to concentrate on yourselves at first. And you should. But I do hope I'll live to see the little ones."

Polly caught her aunt's determined use of the plural. She tensed at the idea of making love with Reid, of nights lying in his arms, his soul-destroying kisses leading to the exquisite sensation of lovemaking with him. Of having his babies growing in her womb.

Martha said, "I want to set aside a gift for my grandniece's and grandnephews' college educations."

With a tremulous smile Polly knelt to hug her aunt. Martha's funds were limited. She lived on Social Security, a small pension from her husband, and the modest income from the interest on a few bonds. By no means was she rich, except in her heart.

Martha wrapped her arms around Polly's neck. Her own smile wobbled as she said, "This means you'll move, dear. Horace and I will miss you."

Polly took both her hands. "No, Aunt Martha. I couldn't leave you. We're not moving. Reid will practice law in town. We've decided to live here. Isn't that right, sweetheart?"

Turning to Reid, Polly saw his jaw tighten, his eyes narrow. She prayed he wouldn't say anything to hurt her aunt.

He didn't. He nodded and said in a gentle, reassuring voice, "That's our plan."

Martha dissolved into tears. She sniffled, rummaging in her purse for her hankie. "My dreams are answered. Forgive a foolish old woman. I'm crying from happiness. Polly, I wish your parents had lived to see this day."

She turned a fond gaze on Reid. "I'm her surrogate mother, you see. I have been since her dear mother passed away. Every mother wants to see her daughter settled in a good marriage. I've been sneaking glances at you when you're looking at Polly, and it's obvious you're devoted to my niece. And your love has been tested. You came back for her."

Polly choked up. "I'll get wine," she said, and fled to the dining room, where she kept a wine rack on the sideboard.

She leaned her forehead against the wall, then jumped when she felt a hand at her shoulder. She whirled around.

Reid stood there. She tipped her head back, her face tight. For once he appeared as disturbed as she felt.

"I hope you're satisfied," she said in frustrated misery. "You drummed up this chicanery. I should never have gone along with it. When you leave, you can have the pleasure of knowing I'll break her heart."

"Then don't tell her. Let her go on thinking we're engaged."

Polly's mouth dropped open.

DON'T HOLD BACK!

1. **No obligation!** No purchase necessary! Enter our Sweepstakes for a chance to win!
2. **FREE!** Get your first shipment of 6 Loveswept books, *and* a lighted makeup case as a free gift.
3. **Save money!** Become a member and about once a month you get 6 books for the price of 4! Return any shipment you don't want.
4. **Be the first!** You'll always receive your Loveswept books before they are available in stores. You'll be the first to thrill to these exciting new stories.

Detach here and mail today.

WINNERS CLASSIC SWEEPSTAKES
Entry Form

YES! I want to see where passion will lead me!

Place FREE ENTRY Sticker Here

Place FREE BOOKS Sticker Here

Enter me in the sweepstakes! I have placed my FREE ENTRY sticker on the heart.

Send me six *free* Loveswept novels *and* my *free* lighted makeup case! I have placed my FREE BOOKS sticker on the heart.

Mend a broken heart. Use both stickers to get the most from this special offer!

61234

NAME_____

ADDRESS_____ APT._____

CITY_____

STATE_____ ZIP_____

Loveswept's Heartfelt Promise to You!

CD211

Give in to love and see where passion leads you!
Enter the Winners Classic Sweepstakes and
send for your FREE lighted makeup case and
6 FREE Loveswept books today!

(See details inside.)

Detach here and mail today.

SEVEN

Polly recovered from her shock in record time. "For how long? Until our twenty-fifth wedding anniversary? Exactly how do I accomplish this miracle with a phantom fiancé? Where do you dream up cons like this? Do they come naturally?"

Reid ground his back teeth. "No, they don't. I should have insisted you follow my orders. But no! Out of the goodness of my heart I thought this up as an alternative."

"So now it's my fault?" she blasted.

He snarled a curse that ripened the air. "As much as it's mine, and don't you forget it. I was for keeping that sweet old lady off the property. If necessary, I'm for yanking out her phone so she can't screw this up by telling the world who I am."

Polly's whole body started to tremble. Her heart twisted in panic. He expected her to continue this absurd charade. She closed her eyes and swallowed.

"We can't stay here arguing. It's begun to rain. After dinner I'd appreciate it if you'd drive Aunt Martha home. You can use my car."

During dinner Martha entertained Reid with stories of Polly as a little girl. Polly finally put an end to it. Undaunted, Martha asked Reid about his family. When she learned that both he and his mother lived in Pittsburgh, and that his mother repaired wicker furniture, she said she wanted to ask her to look at her wicker.

Polly grabbed her glass of wine, tilted it back, and drank it down.

Rain was falling steadily by the time they finished dessert. Polly packed up the leftovers for her aunt, then told her not to go out the next day if it was still raining. She and Reid would visit her instead.

Martha's parting comment was that she planned to write Axl Rose and invite him to the wedding. Why not? Polly thought, slumping back in her chair. Since she'd met Reid, nothing would surprise her.

He was gone for about twenty minutes. When he returned, his expression was somber. Twirling the stem of her wineglass, Polly looked up at him from where she still sat at the kitchen table.

From her perspective he looked formidable. His shoulders were powerful, his thighs hard, his legs long. He wasn't wearing a jacket or a gun at his waist. She could attest to the fact that his stomach was hard and flat. And so was the expression on his face when he saw her sipping a glass of wine.

"Congratulations on your Oscar-winning performance," she said. "You overdid it, don't you think? Dating is one thing. Where do you come off telling her we're engaged?"

"The same place you came off telling her I'm going to practice law in this town and live in this house."

"I had to say something. You left me no choice."

"You might have tried sounding ambiguous."

"Hah." She wiggled her ring finger. "What's your excuse? This isn't ambiguous. I can get arrested for wearing stolen jewelry."

She examined the twinkling solitaire. "Arrested by you! Oh, that's funny. My bogus fiancé steals the ring from a jewel thief, then he puts it on my finger to seal a sham engagement. What happens to my reward? Will it be delivered to me while I'm in jail?"

He shrugged. "The ring leaves when I do. I got caught up in the act. It slipped out."

"I'll say. Until I met you, I lived a nice, quiet, predictable life. I like my routine life. To a man like yourself that's boring. You dismantle bombs. You catch crooks. I catch colds."

He hooked a chair with his foot, slid it backward, and sat. "Colds?"

She nodded. "A metaphor for a normal life. I plan my days, then you barrel into my life and in little more than twenty-four hours we're engaged. Pass the wine bottle, please."

He peered at her. "You've had enough. We're going out."

"I still have to change. You drive me nuts. I've never had a man drive me nuts before."

His lips twitched. "This from a woman of the world."

"We live in different worlds. Either you're kissing me or you're pulling a nutty stunt. My poor aunt. She just relived her romance with my uncle. How could you?"

"You know why. To keep her from telling the world I'm a cop. And there's one more thing you should know."

She dropped her chin on her palm. "Whatever it is will keep until Monday. I'm taking the weekend off. My shock limit is filled."

She started removing the ring, but his hand covered hers. "I'd leave that on if I were you."

She sent him an exasperated look. "No, thanks. There's no reason to keep up this pretense. I've decided to tell Martha the truth."

He fit the ring back on her finger. "You can't tell your aunt."

"Of course I can."

"Even if I allowed it, which I won't, it's too late."

"What do you mean?"

"When I walked your aunt inside her house, she asked me if I was sure that I was leaving Monday or Tuesday. After I said yes, guess what she did? Guess what she's doing even as we speak?"

"I haven't the foggiest idea. What's more, as long as I know she's safely home, my brain is off duty."

"Are you getting drunk?"

"No. I'm nursing a second wine."

"Good," he said with infuriating calm. "I can't have my wife drunk."

She hooted. "Get off it. I'm not your anything. We're not engaged." She pulled off the diamond ring. "I'm breaking our engagement. I believe this bauble is state's evidence."

"Polly," he said flatly. "Put the damn ring on."

Suddenly she understood the look on his face. "You're about to tell me bad news, aren't you?"

"That depends on your definition of bad news."

"Stop trying to soften the blow. Talk!"

He gave her a weak smile that threatened to collapse into laughter. "Take my advice. Stay calm. On a scale of one to ten, it's only about a five."

A sense of foreboding crept up her spine. "What?"

He took a deep breath. "Your aunt Martha's throwing us an engagement party."

Polly shot him an incredulous look. "Tell me you talked her out of it."

"I couldn't. It might blow my cover."

Aghast, she leaped from her chair. "I'm going to strangle you. No! I'll blow your brains out instead. Give me your gun!"

A flicker of humor danced in his eyes. Easily restraining her, he anchored her against his powerful frame. "Be sensible." He nipped her ear.

"Sensible!" The screech turned into a moan as his

tongue bathed the lobe. "When? When is the party? Stop kissing me!"

He chuckled. "I can't. You know what happens when we're together. Brace yourself. Your aunt's a sly fox. She's a faster worker than I am."

"Impossible! No one works faster than you do!"

"She was calling your school-staff list when I left."

Polly squirmed uselessly. Reid was kissing her neck, his breath doing crazy things to her nerves.

"Sunday," he went on. "Even Nature is helping her. The rain should be over by then. We'll have a lovely day for our festivities. Your aunt's calling it my debut. Her word as she kissed me good-bye."

"Heaven help me."

"She showed me lists of names. 'Ooodles of names' is the way she put it. I haven't heard that word in years. *Oodles.* Each 'oodle' is a person. A guest bearing good tidings for our happy future."

"Happy future. You're ruining mine, you louse. You and your award-winning act. Let me go!"

He smiled into her eyes. "Promise not to shoot me?"

She grinned, and he released her. "I'm calling her. Maybe she can reverse the damage before it's too late."

He caught her shoulders. "You'll do nothing of the kind. You'll see this through the same as I will. Your aunt's a terrific woman. I'm not breaking her heart."

"All of a sudden you care. She's my aunt, not yours.

Why didn't you think about her feelings before telling her we're engaged?"

"In my wildest dreams I never thought she'd throw us a party. Incidentally she's decided on having it here. She says your lawn is ideal for a garden party. It's larger and flatter than hers."

Polly let out a yelp. "That can mean only one thing. She's inviting the world. She'll fill every inch of grass with people. Martha knows everyone. How am I going to explain my one-day engagement? People will descend here like an army with feasts of food and good cheer. Not only will she invite them to the wedding, I have no doubt she'll tell them we're having twins in ten months."

He stroked her back in gentle strokes. "Mmmm. I love your perfume. Don't forget the other two kids. It's wrong to play favorites."

She shook her head, trying not to purr at his soothing caresses. "What a miserable mess. I hope Grayson is worth this."

Reid rested his chin atop Polly's head. What he'd hoped was a plausible reason to keep Martha away from danger had snowballed into a huge problem. He had no alternative now.

"I can't let Martha know why I'm here. Let's go out and have some fun. You deserve a break from this tonight. While you dress, I'll check the bridge. When I'm through, I'll change my clothes. I want to go dancing tonight before anything else happens."

The phone rang, and he groaned. "I bet it's your aunt asking me for a list of my friends and relatives."

He was wrong. It wasn't Martha. It was Fran. She sounded strained and upset as she asked to speak with Reid.

Polly handed him the phone, then started loading dishes into the dishwasher. She didn't pay attention to the conversation, but when Reid replaced the phone on its cradle, he was shaking his head, muttering, "It can't be."

Polly glanced at him, but said nothing. Police business didn't interest her at the moment.

He sat down at the table and shook his head. "Brace yourself. I have news."

"You're leaving."

"Hardly."

He seemed to be struggling to keep his face straight.

"Then what?" she asked, drying her hands.

"Fran's stuck."

"What do you mean? How stuck is stuck?"

"I'd say stuck overnight."

Stuck overnight. As in spending the night alone with Reid.

At first Polly thought she heard wrong. "Tell me this isn't true."

"Fran's fiancé's car was rear-ended when he stopped for a light. Tom's home with a neck brace and medication. He says he's okay, but she wants to stay with him. As long as Grayson isn't expected tomorrow, she received permission to be relieved from duty tonight."

Polly felt a bead of perspiration form on her upper lip. Reid picked up her hand, his thumb idly stroking her palm. "It's been an interesting couple of days," he said. "I came here to catch a crook, but what happened? I met you. You refused to tell your aunt to stay away. I'm a nice fellow, so I let you have your way. When I felt guilty for calling off your roofer, I patched your barn roof as best I could. Afterward, I diffused a dynamite charge. The next thing I know I'm engaged and your aunt is throwing us a party. You've told her I'm quitting my job and opening a law practice in a town where I don't know a soul, present company, Martha, Horace, and Cuddles excluded."

He sighed. "If your aunt is right, and pinkies never lie, I'm fathering twins, then a boy and a girl. But do I worry about the price of milk? No. Why should I? Not with Horace ready to do her part. And Martha wants me to draw up a new will for her to bequeath our children money for their college educations."

He massaged his thigh. "Have I summed it up right?"

Hearing his bleak but amusing assessment, seeing the grin tugging at his gorgeous mouth and the devilish light in his eyes, Polly couldn't contain herself. She collapsed into her chair, laughing.

"Except for one thing." She raised her hand, flashing her temporary engagement ring. With an impudent toss of her head, she declared, "Reid Cameron, suh, you're no Ashley Wilkes!"

He leaned forward. Lifting a lock of her hair, he let it slide through his fingers. "But you, my dear, are better than Scarlett."

A pleasant, cozy peace filled the room, while outside rain pelted the ground. Polly made coffee, and they traded stories of their childhoods, especially what it was like for both of them to be only children.

"I learned to depend on myself awfully fast," Polly admitted.

"It's too bad you didn't have a brother or sister. Keeping up this place is a tremendous responsibility."

"There have been times when I've hung on by the skin of my teeth, but it's worth it. The reward money will pay off my bills."

"Then I'm doubly glad I came."

"Doubly?" Her heart skipped a beat. His character, his sense of morality, coupled with his humor and caring, made him more than merely a handsome man. Cuddles trotted over to him and climbed onto his shoe.

Reid took her hand. "You're the first reason."

"Who's coming in Fran's place tonight?"

"No one."

Her pulse skipping, Polly fought to hide her feelings. "No one?"

"That's right," he said with one of his devastating smiles. "It's just us. Would you call this the hand of fate?"

From the moment Reid had walked into her home, Polly thought, Fate had conspired to play tricks on her. Suddenly the atmosphere in the room became highly charged. One thin wall would separate them and the powerful sexual attraction between them. She was a responsible adult, so why should it matter if she had a house full of guests or just one? On the other hand her body reacted to his like a charge of dynamite waiting for ignition.

He swung his foot side by side, giving Cuddles a ride.

"It's raining," he said. "Would you prefer staying home?"

"No! I've got cabin fever."

He put the dog on the floor. "You don't say."

"Mmmm. Yes. A most horrible case. I'm keyed up."

He rose, then bent over her. His long fingers curved around her nape. She saw the brilliant glitter in his eyes, his sensual smile, and she knew he wasn't fooled.

"You mean restless?" he said, drawing her out of the chair and into his arms. There was no mistaking the blatant look of arousal in his eyes.

Polly inhaled his manly scent. Heat radiated between them. He was rapidly becoming too important to her. She swallowed. "Exactly."

He was kissing her ear, his warm breath spiking the level of intimacy to a higher degree. "Martha claims it's destiny."

"Not if we stay out late dancing."

"Silly girl." His mouth was a fraction from hers. "We still have to come back." His voice held a soft but potent promise.

She didn't need him to spell it out. The message in his dark eyes held her mesmerized. *We want each other*, he was saying silently. *You decide.*

Feeling hot and a little breathless, she eased from his embrace. "I'm going up to change."

He let her go, then said, "I'll check the bridge. Where do you keep your flashlight?"

"Can't it wait for daylight? Why grope in the dark?" she argued, bewildered by her need to protect a man who obviously didn't need or want her protection.

"I'd rather not wait until tomorrow. It shouldn't take me long. If I find loose planks, I'll phone headquarters, and they'll send a repair crew tomorrow. We don't want to hamper Grayson from his destination to a jail cell."

Grayson! Of course he'd be uppermost in Reid's mind. She'd gotten the reminder she needed. Reid and Fran, and whoever else was coming from the police department, would arrest the crooks, then Reid would leave. His reminder gave her a much-needed dose of reality.

"There are flashlights on the shelf in the front hall closet. Take one of the umbrellas too. They're in the stand near the front door."

Upstairs, she chose a yellow dress with a scooped neckline, formfitting bodice, and a bias-cut skirt that flared out over her hips for easy dancing. She attached pearl studs to her lobes and brushed out her hair. After slipping into a pair of multicolored-leather strap sandals, she went downstairs.

Despite the rain and darkness, Reid was obviously going over the bridge with a fine-tooth comb. He wouldn't want to call a repair crew out for nothing.

When fifteen minutes had elapsed, her excuses rang thin in her ears. She was worried. Changing her sandals for running shoes, she grabbed a flashlight and an umbrella and hurried out to look for him. The wind whipped at her back. She angled the umbrella to protect her face from pinpoints of driving rain. The flashlight barely cut through the gloom of the night.

"Reid!" she called, sweeping the light before her.

She was met by silence. She called his name again. Silence. Worry etched its way up her spine. Could Grayson have slipped through the police net? Could he be holding Reid prisoner? Spears of genuine alarm knotted her muscles. Reid would have answered her if he could.

She was halfway across the bridge when she spotted him. "Ohmigod!"

She felt the blood drain from her face. Her heart pounded mercilessly. No wonder he hadn't answered. He had fallen through the bridge; only his upper torso was visible. His arms braced on planks on either side, he was trying to free himself. Each time he moved, the wooden planks groaned.

"Stay back!" he warned. Rain spattered his head and dripped down his face.

She halted, panic gripping her. It would have been hard for him to hang on in dry weather, but with rain-slippery hands, it required superhuman effort. Sudden pressure or one false move threatened his precarious position.

Polly couldn't stand idle. If he tumbled into the swollen river, he risked crashing onto one of the many boulders directly below. If he was maimed—or God forbid died!—she wouldn't be able to live with herself. She took a step forward on rubbery legs.

"Don't!" Reid yelled. "For God's sake, don't try to save me."

"What can I do?"

"Pray I don't fall through and hurt my precious hide."

His feeble attempt at humor plummeted her into despair. Assailed by guilt, she assumed full responsibility for his accident. With each scant inch of freedom he gained, she agonized. With each breath he labored, hers expelled in strangled hope. Biting down hard on her lip, she mentally shared his terrible ordeal.

The wrenching sounds of wood echoed in the night as he tried to shimmy backward. Only his lower legs remained hidden now. Adjusting the angle of his torso, he freed more of his legs.

She shone her light to aid him. "Reid, I see what you can't. The planks can't hold your weight much longer. Don't fight me. Please, darling. It's your only chance."

She closed her umbrella and dropped it on the bridge. Getting down on her knees, she crawled over to him, positioning herself behind him. From his grunts and groans she couldn't begin to imagine what the pain of hanging on was doing to his back muscles, in addition to his legs and groin.

He offered a feeble protest. "Go away. We'll both go down. Let me do this myself."

"Argue later," she said as she slid her arms under his and around his chest. "You saved my life in the hayloft doing this. Now, hush, darling. I know what to do."

He eased his grip, allowing her to pull him backward. When they felt solid wood beneath them, he sat motionless while Polly crawled around to the hole to help free his feet.

She lay down at right angles to his legs. Reaching forward, she gently freed one foot, then the other. Reid braced himself on his elbows, angling his body away from the hole.

When both legs were free, she scooted back and

grabbed him under the shoulders again. With his help she pulled him toward safety. Drenched and panting, she clung to him, rocking with him, shielding him with her body.

He pushed the thick wet strands of hair from her face. She was weeping, raining kisses of joy over his face.

"I owe you my life," he said hoarsely.

"Thank God, you're safe," she murmured over and over, the shock of his near death setting in as the splintering sound of wood being released from its mooring tore through the night.

She shuddered. Reid had come within a hairsbreadth of hurtling to his death. "If not for my stubbornness, you wouldn't be hurt."

"Don't blame yourself. I should have been more careful."

His attempt to suppress a groan knifed her heart. She didn't have time to waste. "I'm taking you off this bridge, out of the rain, or you'll get pneumonia."

"Help me up."

"I've got a better idea. There's a flatbed cart near the barn, the one with the long wooden handles. You'll ride back."

He shivered, and she hugged him more tightly. "You can't pull me," he said. "I'm okay. I'll walk."

"Horace!" she cried in a fit of brilliance. "You saved her from drenching her hooves and from being blown to smithereens. The least she can do is help you in an emergency."

Refusing further discussion, she dashed for the umbrella, sprang it open, shoved the handle in his hand, then ran toward the barn.

"Horace," Reid muttered. Rescue by a cow would have brought a smile to his lips if not for his aching muscles, exacerbated by the dull throb in his thigh. He'd cut himself on his sore leg. Cursing his rotten luck, he waited for Polly.

Light-headed, he thought for a minute he was losing it, when he heard an ungodly noise. As it grew louder and louder, he identified the source of the racket.

"In a million years," he said aloud, "the guys would never believe this."

Polly, an adorable, bedraggled, defiant angel, her dress and hair plastered to her, was walking toward him lugging Horace's makeshift reins. The incredible sight reminded him of a marching band gone haywire. Polly led the cow onto the bridge, leaving her where she knew it was safe. Horace's bell clanged to the accompaniment of Guns N' Roses.

Reid stood up. "Tell me I don't have to listen to that."

"Horace refuses to budge otherwise. You know she hates getting her hooves wet. Good thing I keep a battery-powered tape recorder in the barn in case of power outtages."

Leaning heavily on Polly, Reid made his way to the cart. With effort they managed to get him in it, then Polly turned Horace around, and they headed for the house.

Reid wished she'd thought to bring him some ear-plugs.

"Do you think anything's broken?" Polly asked as she helped him down from the cart.

"Nothing's broken. The legs are fine. I'm okay." He caught her worried expression. "Believe me, I've had worse. A hot shower will fix me up in no time."

Her expression guarded, she wrapped an arm around his waist and helped him into the house. Once inside, she eyed the staircase.

"Reid, I can bring down a mattress. But if you decide you'd rather sleep down here, I'd have to put the mattress on the floor. In this old house that's drafty. And if you need to use the bathroom during the night, it would be hard for you to get up. Personally I think, if you can make it upstairs, you should. You can take a soothing shower, then lie down. You'd be better off in my king-size bed too."

Hearing her nervous babbling, watching her bite her lips, he knew she didn't think much of his chances of making it upstairs. "Polly, stop worrying. Of course I can manage the stairs. I'll take a hot shower, and I'll be fine. Just give me a second to recoup my energy."

While he mobilized his strength, Polly raced upstairs, flipping on lights. She whipped off the bedspread and yanked down the covers on her bed, then flew into the bathroom. Turning on the shower, she left the shower door open a crack so the steam could warm the room. She set out clean, thick terry-cloth towels and a washcloth, along with a bottle of peroxide and a box of Band-Aids. As she sped downstairs, she was amazed at how well she was coping with the change from her routine life to a life that was unpredictable and more eventful than anything she'd ever known. She was changing in ways she'd never expected, not the least of which were her turbulent emotions.

Reid finished his long, hot shower, the soothing water easing the muscle strain as he'd thought it would. After drying himself, he put on a clean pair of briefs, then leaned against the washstand in Polly's pink-and-white tile bathroom. Before he'd used the bathroom without loitering, but now he took stock of Polly's personal items. Lady's shaver, deodorant, lipsticks, mascara, brushes. Bubble bath and bath powder sat on the counter. Nice feminine things. Not one sign of a male occupant, which suggested that no man shared her bedroom on a permanent basis. Not that it was his right, but the thought pleased him.

He glanced in the mirror. "Cameron, you look like hell."

He closed the lid on the toilet and sat down, then reached for the bottle of peroxide. Immediately he shouted in pain.

"What's wrong?" Polly yelled from the other side of the door. She had just come from her bedroom, where she had changed into her nightgown and robe.

"Nothing," he answered. "I'm okay."

"Are you decent?"

"Yes."

She opened the door, and her eyes swiftly examined him. He was wearing next to nothing—not exactly what she would call "decent." She couldn't help staring at his wide shoulders, at the line of dark hair that veed down his broad chest and disappeared inside his underwear. She had never seen such a lean, hard, magnificent body.

Not even in her dreams.

He looked wonderful. With a trembling smile she laid one hand on his cheek, trying to offer solace. He turned his face into her hand and sighed.

"I swiveled to grab the peroxide to pour on the cut. Don't mind me. When it comes to pain, I'm a coward."

"You are not," she said stoutly. "You're the bravest man I know. Here, I'll do it."

As she bent over him, she saw a small scar on his thigh. "What caused this?"

When he didn't answer, her breath caught. Dawning awareness had her looking up.

"You were the cop who stopped the bullet, weren't you?"

"Yes."

"I saw you rubbing your thigh today. You were hurting before the accident."

"Twinging," he amended, with a tenderness that melted her heart. He was trying to comfort her. Her eyes stung.

"After all I've put you through, I'm not letting you lift a finger."

"The shower took the pain away. This was just a twinge. I'm fine. I want you to know that under fire you're marvelous. You saved my life."

"Marvelous." Her voice quavered. "I'm so marvelous I nearly got you killed. I'm so marvelous, I disregarded your warning."

In his line of work Reid had seen people collapse under stress. A trembling Polly tore at his heart in ways he'd never before felt. Taking her hands, he drew them away from her face. Tears glistened in her eyes.

"Don't," he murmured huskily. "It's okay. I'll prove it. We'll go dancing tomorrow night."

"Oh, please! We both know why I suggested that. Now look what I've done. I've rendered you useless."

He grinned. The result of her nearness was plainly evident. "Better take another look."

An embarrassed flush crept up her cheeks. "You know what I mean."

He touched her face, idly brushing his thumb over her cheek. "Will you dry my hair, please?"

Obviously attempting to dispel the sexual tension

rising between them, she dried his hair vigorously, first by toweling it, then with the blow dryer. After fluffing his hair with her fingers, she stepped back to observe her handiwork.

"There. I'm through."

He caught her wrist, pulling her closer. A feeling of intimacy pervaded the steam-filled room. "You really haven't met a braver man?"

"Absolutely not, darling. You're as brave, if not braver, than Rhett Butler." She winked. "Far braver than Ashley Wilkes."

He rewarded her with a broad smile. "Good, I like that."

In the bedroom he asked for the phone that sat on a table near a wing chair. He needed to report to his headquarters. After talking for a few minutes, he covered the mouthpiece of the phone and told her a crew would fix the bridge in the morning.

"Any new developments?" he said, returning to his phone conversation. He was given the latest on Grayson's movements. He had arrived at his girl-friend's house. The police would arrive at Polly's Monday to seal off the exits and help with Grayson's arrest.

Reid hung up. "Everything's under control. There's nothing to worry about."

She took a deep breath. "I'm so grateful you're all right, Reid. If anything had happened to you . . ." She choked up for a moment. "I'll say good night."

"No, please don't go. Stay." His intense gaze held her as forcefully as his softly spoken appeal. "Stay."

He held out his hand.

She nodded and took the steps her heart couldn't deny. When she sat on the edge of the bed, Reid lifted her hand and kissed it. His were strong hands, she thought, capable of diffusing a dynamite charge, or of tenderly stroking her as he was doing now.

Rain beat at the windows, but there, in the confines of her canopied bed, nothing mattered but Reid. A lock of dark hair had fallen over his forehead. Giving in to her impulse, she pushed it off his forehead, then kissed his temple.

"I'm having a wide-awake dream," he murmured.

Her gaze roved over his face. The stark raw emotion she read in his eyes compelled her to ask, "Is it a good dream?"

"The best. In it we're making love."

"Are we, darling?" She felt her senses awakening as his thumb languorously brushed the pulse point on her wrist. Could he feel her heartbeat leap?

"Polly," he said, his voice low and throbbing with intensity. "You can't possibly want me as much as I want you."

She could have told him he was wrong, that her heart was bursting with love for him, but she didn't. Instead, she pushed the thought of sad tomorrows from her mind. He hadn't lied by offering commitments or by pretending to have fallen in love with her. He wanted her. She wanted him. In two days they'd lived through more than most people faced in a lifetime, and they'd triumphed together.

Reid looked up into her beautiful face, at her eyes fringed with thick lashes, at her luscious red lips that tasted like fine wine. He craved her with a surging passion greater than any he'd ever felt before in his life. In a humbling realization he knew why. His overwhelming need stemmed from more than his heated desire to join his body with hers. She had touched his soul.

"Will you share the dream with me?" he asked.

His searing gaze reflected Polly's innermost feelings. From the first she'd felt the sparks of electricity between them. She placed her hand in his, giving him her answer.

EIGHT

"Polly." Reid whispered her name on a sigh of benediction. Kissing her hand, he shifted onto his side, making room for her as she lay down beside him.

"Now I understand the passage I read from your book," he murmured, enfolding her welcoming warmth in his arms.

Polly's heart swelled with tenderness. She stroked his bare chest, kissing the hard, flat planes of his body where her fingers left their sensitive trail. "I was so afraid for you."

He tilted up her chin and kissed away her tears. "Shhh. That's over. We'll celebrate life. Together."

As she slipped off her robe and nightgown, he lit the lamp on the nightstand. Then his arms encircled her naked form, and his mouth met hers in a searing, erotic kiss that sent sparks of pleasure through her.

Cradling her face, he said hoarsely, "It's already better than my dream." His heated gaze traveled down her slim body.

"You're beautiful," he murmured, kissing her lips. He scattered kisses down her body, not letting her hide any part of it from his view or taste.

Astounded by her feelings, she pulled him close, burying her face against his shoulder, kissing him there and on his neck.

Igniting her with fire, claiming her for his, his hands swept over her body. He cupped the nest of curls at the apex of her thighs, and she arched upward, pressing against his palm.

She ran her hands down his arms, then sank her hands in his hair. As he slipped one finger inside her dewy, pulsing flesh, she moaned with pleasure.

She reached for his hard shaft, stroking him and heightening both their needs.

It was his turn to moan. Even as he pleasured her, she was driving him wild. He trailed kisses along her cheek and neck, before returning to devour her lips. Their tongues tangled, while his hand shaped her breast. He shifted her upward, his rougher skin branding hers. When he took her breast in his mouth, sucking first one nipple, then the other, her body vibrated with a response greater than any she'd thought possible.

A liquefying heat flowed to the pit of her stomach as he tormented her with exquisite mastery, worshiping her with his mouth and touch. Just when she thought she couldn't take more, he wrapped his arms around her, holding her flush to his naked body, giving her a brief respite before beginning his tender assault again, showering her with adoration.

His hands played over her silken skin, driving her upward, higher and higher, until she writhed in his arms, begging for release. "Reid . . . now, please. Together."

He reached for the packet of protection he'd placed on her nightstand. After slipping the sheath on, he shifted on top of her. Wanting to go slow, reining back his instinctive need to take her in one long thrust, he entered her by degrees. But when she clutched his hips and clamped her legs around his waist so that she could take all of him, he slipped past the point of self-control. Again and again, he thrust into her, burying himself fully, feeling her inner muscles tighten their hold, contracting, quivering.

And then he could hold back no longer. Drugged on her alluring scent, her thrilling kisses, the wine that was Polly, he drove into her heat. With bodies pressed close, with lips kissing, with hands eliciting sighs of rapture, Reid's hoarse shout rumbled from deep within his soul. Hurled into her own blinding explosion, Polly cried out too.

Reid bowed his head beside hers. "This is our dream, Polly," he whispered. "No one else's."

Much later, when their breathing had calmed and their world had tilted upright again, he shifted to his side, still joined to her in an intimate embrace. She gazed at him, and in the afterglow of love, his words came back to her.

This is our dream, Polly. No one else's.

Dreams, she knew, were fleeting, forgotten in the light of day. For now she wouldn't think of tomorrow. Snuggling in his arms, she kissed his cheek. She understood exactly what he had meant.

Awake, Reid lay on his side, his hand drifting over a sleeping Polly's hip to slide upward and cup her breast. She sighed contentedly. What a surprise, he thought, thinking of this amazing woman who snuggled against him. Making love with her affected him to his core. She enriched him, made him feel as if he were ten feet tall, a better human being than he was. After their lovemaking had ended, he'd half expected her to talk about the future, one that included him. She hadn't.

She had smiled at him, kissed him softly on the lips, thanked him for letting her share his lovely dream, then teasingly commented he had a radiant look in his eyes. He hadn't been surprised. She'd bowled him over. From the first moment they'd met, sparks flew around them. Yet she seemed to accept their lovemaking as simply a celebration of life, a culmination of the intense attraction they felt toward each other, coupled with the dangers they'd faced.

What should he say? Making no demands, she'd touched his soul. Always before when he'd made love, it had ended with satisfaction. With Polly he'd reached the heights of heaven. And now what?

Now he went on with his life. Polly was more than a dream. They were lovers. They faced a farce of an engagement party, where he'd mingle with people who loved her and would wish them well. Martha would be in her glory, fluttering among her guests, introducing him to everyone.

No matter how noble his intentions, he was in a mess of his own making. He didn't want to think about Grayson or the hurt Martha would feel when she learned why they'd set up this ruse. But if they didn't tell Martha, then she, Polly's co-workers, and everyone else they'd meet would think they were engaged. How could they develop a normal relationship in the face of that? The answer was, they couldn't.

Polly stirred. "Can't you sleep?" she murmured drowsily. "Would you rather I leave?"

"No. That's the one thing I don't want. Shhh, go back to sleep."

Gathering her closer, he nuzzled her neck. She sighed deeply, snuggled against him, then drifted back to sleep.

In minutes he joined her, breathing her delightful scent.

At 6:30 A.M. Polly eased Reid's arm off her breast and slipped out of bed. Much as she hated leaving the warm cocoon, Horace awaited her. As soon as she'd awakened, the reality of her feelings for Reid had threatened to overwhelm her. She needed time to put them into perspective so she could steer her life back onto its safe, normal course. The first thing to do was put last night into focus. By acting adult about it, not making more of it than it was, she could lessen the pangs of loneliness she would feel after Reid left.

Who was she kidding?

She loved him. When love was one-sided, it was doomed to end. Last night she'd made the decision to spend the night with him, to make love with him. Though she knew she'd have to let him go, she wouldn't change a single loving moment they had shared. She would never find such closeness of spirit with anyone but Reid.

Silently gathering her clothes, she paused to look at him. With his hair tousled, the blanket slipped down to expose his broad chest, he appeared as sexy as he did when he was awake, and that was saying something. Maybe it was because they'd been intimate. When he woke up and looked at her, she knew his dark eyes would fill with heated memory, reminding her that only a few hours earlier, he had made love to her for a second time.

Even as she watched him, his hand snagged her pillow. Wrapping his arms around the pillow, he burrowed his face in it and slept on.

So noise from the bathroom wouldn't awaken him, she washed and dressed in the kitchen. After making a pot of coffee, she headed for the barn.

Either Horace wasn't in the mood to fuss, or she was unusually happy to see Polly. Polly was able to milk her without benefit of music, then Horace lumbered docilely out to the pasture.

The morning was flawless, making last night's danger seem surreal. A slight breeze shook raindrops from tree leaves. The cool morning temperature would rise into the high 70s. She made her way over to the bridge, surveying its span as she walked onto it. She remained clear of the section that had nearly claimed Reid for a victim. Her heart constricted when she thought of his close call.

Retracing her steps, she walked home. In the kitchen she poured a mug of coffee for Reid and went upstairs to her bedroom. After setting the mug down on the dresser, she drew the curtains aside. Sun streamed through the windows.

Reid stirred and blinked. "Mmmm. I like waking up and seeing you."

"Do you?" she murmured.

"Yes. Is that coffee for me?"

She brought it over. "I'm glad to see you've regained your health."

"Thanks to last night's special treatment. Have you milked Horace this morning?"

She nodded.

"Then you're free?"

"Yes."

He kicked aside the light blanket and lay naked in

her bed, a magnificent, fully aroused male animal. As his heated gaze singed her with undesigned longing, he all but declared he wanted to devour her in the most succulent way. "Let's not waste the best part of the morning then."

Polly's breath caught. They had so little time left. She wondered if he could see everything she felt for him in her eyes. Her hands went to the buttons on her blouse.

"No," he said. "Come here. I want to do that."

He turned the simple act of removing her clothes into an erotic experience, kissing her breasts, laving her skin, awakening erogenous zones until she writhed in his arms, begging him to take her.

He brought his mouth down on hers. She met him in a demanding kiss. Reid felt the warmth of her lips in pleasurable torment. The breath hissed out of him when she also cupped him intimately. Her kisses, her touch, roared him to life, slamming into his loins with unbearable tension.

They made love on rumpled sheets with the sun warming their bodies. They showed each other exactly how and where to please, discovering even more pleasure than they'd found the night before.

"I love the feel and taste of your body," Reid murmured. He kissed her greedily, then traced the tip of his tongue around a nipple. "You like this?"

"You know I do," she said, arching against him.

He buried his face between the sweet valley of her

breasts, and she shuddered, delighting him with her response. Swiftly he prepared himself, then entered her. She met his driving strokes with a sense of urgency, and he wondered if she, like himself, was achingly aware that in a few days they would go their separate ways. To do otherwise meant continuing the fabrication that they were engaged, and the stress would be unfair to both of them.

He made love to her fiercely, sweeping her into their special sensory world. Polly surrendered to him completely, letting him take her soaring to the highest peak. But when she floated down, she rolled away so he couldn't see the tears in her eyes.

He gathered her in his arms. "Did you know you called me *darling*, both last night and this morning?"

"Yes," she whispered.

He kissed her shoulder. "Words of endearment are common for engaged couples."

Or couples in love, she could have added. Reid was offering her an out, though, a polite way for her to state the obvious.

She did. "We're not engaged. If I tell Martha about the bridge, it gives us and her an excuse to cancel her party. What do you think?"

Subdued by her suggestion, Reid was silent for a minute. The bridge did offer a plausible and perfect excuse to cancel the party. So why wasn't he leaping to agree with her? Polly's reasoning was as sound as his. Why wasn't he urging her to make the phone call?

He saw himself playing the intended bridegroom, kissing and hugging Polly, grinning and shaking hands with the people congratulating him. While the idea was attractive, the subterfuge wasn't. Polly deserved better. Like her, it disturbed him. But what really agitated him was lying next to her, spent from their loving, and thinking about their impending separation. Could he really give her up?

"I think it would be unwise to cancel," he said.

She frowned down at him. "I've got a lot to lose, Reid. First, my friends meet you, then they hold my hand when I tell them we called it off. It's wrong."

"Your aunt won't cancel. She'll postpone the party. Last night she asked me for a list of my friends and relatives. I told her not to bother, that no one would be able to make it on such short notice. If she postpones the party, though, she'll want to call them. It adds another wrinkle."

"It's all the more reason to phone her and tell her the engagement's off. That eliminates complications."

"I dislike secretiveness as much as you, but your aunt's blabbed to half the town. So that's out for now."

Polly felt on the brink of hysteria. She couldn't be as dispassionate as Reid. Why couldn't she see it from his practical point of view?

She couldn't because she was in love with him.

"Then you want to go through with the pretense?" she asked.

"I do," he replied, regarding her closely. "I don't think we have a choice. When I said that Martha would reschedule the party for next weekend, I thought you understood. By then we'll have captured Grayson."

"And you'll be gone."

"Yes."

She struggled to keep her voice impersonal, as if she were negotiating a business deal. "Okay. We'll do it your way. We'll get through the day. I hope people won't bring presents, but if they do, I'll return them."

Reid got up. "We should dress. Much as I wish the bridge remained impassable so I could have you to myself, I know that's impossible. The construction crew should arrive soon. Also, I've got to hide a camera in the loft, so we can record Grayson in all his thieving glory. When he comes here, I want you to remain in the house. I know you have this tendency to save my life, but don't interfere. By the time he arrives, this place will be swarming with cops."

And that, Polly told herself, was how Reid switched back to being a cop on duty.

Later, when she and Reid were in the kitchen, she phoned her aunt. She told Martha about the unsafe bridge, assured her both she and Reid were fine, and added that a crew would arrive soon to repair the bridge.

"The important thing is that you're both okay," Martha said. "Oh, Polly, we're going to have a marvel-ous time tomorrow. There's no rain in the forecast."

"Aunt Martha, how many people do you expect?" She prayed Martha would say ten or so, fifteen at the most, but somehow she knew the number would be far higher.

"Sixty. Maybe more. It's short notice."

"My Lord!" Polly sank down in a chair. She hadn't dreamed so many would attend. "You made over sixty phone calls! How was that possible without staying up for hours?"

"I didn't make all the calls myself," Martha said. "I phoned Grace, Joan, and Lonni. They were as amazed as I was. You never told anyone about Reid."

Martha giggled. "Grace bet he's slight of build, with blond wispy hair, like Ashley Wilkes. I didn't tell her he's more the Rhett Butler type. I'm saving it for a surprise."

Polly groaned.

"Anyway, I let your friends split up the names on the snow list rather than try to contact everyone myself. Then I phoned the head of the PTA."

"Oh!"

"Oh, yes, and I gave the girls permission to ask the parents of your past and present students. I called your principal myself. What a nice man!"

The room swam before Polly's eyes. "You called Mr. Grant?"

"You're excited, aren't you, darling girl? I can hear it in your voice. It's to be expected. Mr. Grant volunteered to phone his ex-secretary. He said she likes you very much. He wouldn't miss the party, so I told him to bring his wife. As long as it's outdoors on your lawn and the weather's predicted to be great, the more the merrier. Everyone's offered to bring some food. Tell Reid the tables and chairs will arrive tomorrow morning."

Polly shook her head. Her aunt might as well announce it on the local TV station. "What tables and chairs?" she asked weakly.

"The ones I rented, which Reid insisted on paying for."

"He what?" She covered the mouthpiece and whispered to Reid, "You didn't tell me you offered to pay for the tables and chairs. She's invited at least sixty people!"

Martha's happy voice brought her back to the phone. "Grace is giving you a bridal shower. It's no surprise. Pick a suitable date. I told her at the rate you two got yourselves engaged, to expect a wedding soon."

Polly's neck muscles went into spasm.

"Don't worry," Martha added. "She knows you're not pregnant."

Polly's mouth dropped open. Standing, she shoved the phone into Reid's hand.

"Talk to my aunt."

Reid tried not to laugh at Polly's disgruntled expression as Martha asked if Polly was taking good care of him. Maintaining a solemn tone, he assured

Martha he'd never had more personalized or more loving attention in his life.

After he'd hung up, Polly sat back down at the table. "The world is coming here tomorrow," she said, sounding totally demoralized. "This has gotten thoroughly out of hand."

Privately he agreed with her. Aloud he said, "The numbers may make it easier. This way Martha will drag me from group to group. I won't be stuck in long conversations."

"Her short conversations are damaging. I guarantee you she'll announce our four future children."

"I'll stop her."

"Good luck. If you can, you're the first."

"I'll tell her beforehand we feel it's too personal."

"Aunt Martha has got a great batting average with her predictions, and she likes to let people know that."

Reaching across the table, he rubbed his knuckles against her soft cheek. "She'll listen to me. She wouldn't do anything to hurt you. For the record, Polly, you're an intelligent, caring, loving woman. I think you'll make a wonderful mother."

"Let's make breakfast," she said briskly.

While they did, Reid kept talking to Polly, offering reasons why the large numbers of guests would help, not hinder. She noticed that he acted as if it was all in a day's work, a day that would pass quickly. As she made pancakes, he set the table and poured orange juice in their glasses. He disappeared outside for a minute, then came back with a rose he had plucked from the bush near the back door. Her spirits lifted. She couldn't blame him for his honest feelings. Why should she expect him to pretend he was in love with her?

During breakfast Cuddles trotted in and took up his position on Reid's shoe. Reid wiggled his foot, and the dog wrapped his front legs around Reid's ankle. Laughing, Reid asked, "Does Cuddles act this way with everyone?"

Polly smiled. "I've never seen him do it before. He loves you."

"Smart dog."

When he'd finished eating, Reid played with Cuddles. He swung his foot from side to side, giving the dog a ride and laughing when Cuddles wagged his tail like a metronome. Their play was interrupted by a knock at the back door, followed by a voice familiar to Reid.

Cuddles growled when Reid put him on the floor so he could greet his friend Jim Hager, who often worked with the state police. Reid introduced Jim and Polly, and the three left the house. When Reid unthinkingly started to put his arm around Polly, she stepped to the side, shaking her head.

Swearing under his breath, he took note of Polly's subtle warning. He shoved his hands into his pockets, knowing it wouldn't be right for Jim to see him with his arm around a woman while he was on duty. Not only had he forgotten his professional restraint by automatically reaching for Polly, it had felt right and natural to do it. Still, he owed it to Polly not to leave her with emotional baggage. He just wished he didn't feel so rotten about all this subterfuge.

They walked out onto the bridge, toward where Jim's crew was setting up. When they reached the gaping hole, Jim asked Reid how he'd managed to avoid falling.

Reid looked down at the boulders and rushing water beneath the hole. Had he crashed onto one of those rocks, he'd be maimed or dead.

"Polly pulled me to safety. The weather was awful. Besides the rain making it hard for me to hang on and to see, the two of us were soaking wet. Without her I doubt if I could have made it."

Jim looked from Reid to Polly. "He owes you a lot."

Thinking of all they had shared in the past two days, Polly disagreed. Her senses were attuned to Reid, and she was aware of him on so many levels; his scent, the size of him, which made her feel cherished and feminine, the texture of his skin, the way his eyes lit up when he teased her, or darkened in passion. "No, it's I who owe him. I should have had the bridge inspected."

The look Reid gave her said he understood and shared the depth of her feelings. Despite her silent warning to him a few minutes earlier, she was tempted to take his hand. A loud hello forestalled her. Glancing up, they saw Martha at the foot of the bridge, waving. Reid casually pulled the tail of his dark shirt out of his trousers to conceal his gun. Polly sent him a grateful look.

"How long do you think you'll be, Jim?" he asked.

"Can't say for sure. If we can't finish today, we'll shore up the bridge and return later. We'll leave it safe for you, Polly."

"Will we be able to drive across the bridge?" Reid asked. "From what I've seen thus far, the damage seems confined to one area."

Polly saw her aunt start walking toward them and squeezed Reid's arm. "Martha's coming."

They excused themselves, leaving Jim to return to his work. Reid shouted to Martha to stay where she was. Polly knew he was thinking the same thing she was. Jim knew Reid was a state policeman. If Martha joined them, he might, in the course of conversation, allude to Reid's profession, unaware Reid wanted it kept secret.

Martha was a colorful sight in a bright red dress and a fringed red shawl Polly had given her for her birthday. As Polly and Reid reached her, she raised up on tiptoes, craning her head to see what the men were doing.

"Are you certain they'll finish today?" Martha asked.

"I've been assured they'll do their best," Polly

answered. "So far it looks like it's nothing more than replacing loose boards from one section."

"How did you manage to get them here on such short notice?"

Polly gazed at Reid. "Reid knows the right people to call in an emergency."

"You're so lucky, Polly," Martha said.

I wish I were, Polly thought.

"Aunt Martha," Reid said, obviously wanting to change the subject, "you've been busy. I hear you've invited an army."

She playfully poked his arm. "How many times will I get to give my niece an engagement party? I'm not through. This morning I phoned a few friends. We don't have a snow list like Polly's school does, but we have our own grapevine."

"Really."

"Yes. Most of us are widows. We check up on each other. All I did was ask a few friends to call around, then let me know who can come. Everyone is dying to meet you, Reid. Isn't it wonderful? In no time at all you'll be part of our community."

Polly was absorbed in looking at a flock of lucky blackbirds flying overhead. She felt an overpowering urge to learn to fly so she could join the birds as they headed toward the horizon. People adored her aunt, tiny, good-hearted tornado that she was. Hordes of guests, ready to cheer, eat, and be merry would descend there tomorrow, not wanting to disappoint Martha.

Martha went on. "I know there's an overabundance of lawyers today, but not in this part of the state. Parents send their kids to law school, and you'll never guess where those ingrates practice law today."

"Where?" Reid asked.

"Beverly Hills and Seattle. Don't worry about drumming up trade. I'll tell everyone the reason you're moving to our town is out of love for Polly. My friends will be impressed. Then I'll drop the hint that it's time to update their wills."

Polly caught Reid's grim smile. The longer Martha prattled, the more fantastic ideas she came up with. Polly was having some bizarre ideas herself of what the engagement party would be like.

Huge numbers of women would cram into her kitchen, carrying platters of food, with their battle slogan: "This dessert needs refrigeration!"

With the ground muddy in places, her floors would be a mess. Cuddles would be in an excited dither. Which, now that she thought about it, was the least of her worries. She envisioned a long procession of vans from the Let's Party Rental parked in her driveway. Drivers and helpers would set up banquet-size tables and hundreds of folding chairs on the grass. Not to mention a sea of colorful umbrellas and the matching paper goods Martha must have ordered. As commander in chief, Martha would direct her troops, transforming her yard into a magical party.

"Toilet paper," Polly mumbled. "I'll run out of toilet paper."

Martha heard her. "It's taken care of."

Polly muttered thanks.

All Reid could do was stare at the diminutive lady who was cheerfully turning his life upside down. But when he thought she had finally run out of steam, she patted his arm and said the worst thing he could hear.

"Reid, it's only right I contact your dear mother. I'd never forgive myself otherwise. If she can't attend, at least I will have done my duty."

"I'll tell her," he said quickly. "Save you a phone call."

"No," Martha said adamantly. "It's my obligation to issue the invitation. I'm the hostess. Etiquette demands it. Trust me."

Her little hands created tiny windmills as she wound up to ram home her point. "Polly's parents would never forgive me."

"They're dead," Reid said. Forgetting Jim might be watching, he swept his arm around Polly's shoulders, more for support than out of affection.

"In this life," Martha said, "but not in the hereafter. Polly's parents are watching you from heaven this minute."

Reid blanched.

"You think they see everything we did—I mean do?" he asked.

Martha missed his strangled innuendo. "Of course

I do. Let them enjoy their only child's engagement party as much as you two dears will."

Polly's knees buckled. She grabbed on to Reid.

Martha produced a pad and pencil from her pocket and handed it to him with a flourish. "Write down your mother's phone number."

Martha had him, and Reid knew it. To refuse would be rude, and it would hurt her feelings. He scratched the number across the pad.

"It's best if you phone her this afternoon," he said. "She's usually out in the mornings."

"Thank you. If I think of anything else later on, I'll call you." Martha gaily took off like a gyro.

Polly and Reid gaped at each other. Since she couldn't sprout wings, Polly very sincerely wished for the ground to open and swallow her up.

"What a little dynamo." Reid said. "The president should appoint her to his cabinet. Who can say no to her?"

"Not many. When Martha calls, people adjust their prior plans if at all possible. There isn't anyone she hasn't done a favor for over the years. She has a heart of gold."

"I've got to speak with my mother first."

"Make sure she doesn't come."

"That goes without saying. But can you imagine her surprise if she isn't prepared for Martha's phone call?"

Polly couldn't.

NINE

Polly tried to find a silver lining in her aunt's enthusiasm. As she walked away, she glanced at the mountains and the surrounding countryside and its spectacular palette of rippling shades. All right, she scolded herself. The party was one day out of her life. If she didn't dwell on its ramifications, she'd do fine. If the charade got too tough to handle, she could always escape to the pasture, hide out with Horace for a few minutes.

"Can you imagine anything nuttier?" she muttered to Reid.

He inhaled harshly. "Yes, as a matter of fact I can."

She looked at him pleadingly. "What?"

"It'll come to me. Give me a few minutes."

The joke fell flat. They walked on in a somber mood with no particular destination in mind. Finally they ended up at the old apple orchard. Polly perched on a large boulder at one end of the orchard while Reid leaned against a tree.

"This is awful," she said. "All of it. Martha's enthusiasm. The party. Telling your mother. I wish I could take it back or make it go away."

She looked up at him. "We should plan a counteroffensive."

"What do you have in mind?"

"How do I know? This is your department, not mine."

"I'm fresh out of counteroffensives," he said tightly. "It's one thing to need a cover story, but who expected this?" He rubbed a hand across his knotted forehead. "I never involve my mother in my affairs."

Polly rested her chin on her hand. "I don't know why you're complaining. Your mother knows you're in law enforcement. How can telling her this is a charade, a cover for your protection, bother her?"

He grimaced. "I'm not in the habit of lying, so it bothers me. How do you think I feel about Martha throwing us a party?"

Polly shrugged. "You can't possibly feel as rotten as I do."

"I do. I feel like a louse. Once my mother knows the reason I'm asking her to go along with this, she'll start thinking like a mother. She'll empathize with us, but she'll also put herself in Martha's place and wonder why we didn't come up with a better ruse."

"Why *you* didn't come up with a better ruse. Leave me out of this."

He didn't answer, and she shook her head.

"Oh, hell, I'm sorry I said that. I'm as culpable as you. Please forgive me."

He smiled at her. "You're an unusual woman, Polly Sweet. Would you think I'm out of bounds if I asked you to kiss me, just to take the edge off my worries?"

Grinning, she got up and walked over to him, pressing her body to his. As she slid her hands around his neck and raised her face to meet his lips, she decided that the riskiest situations could have a silver, if temporary, lining.

Then she stopped thinking as she threw herself into the kiss. His body warmed from the sun pressed into hers. His hands roamed over her buttocks, urging her closer to his male hardness.

He groaned when she slid her own hand between them to find him. "You're driving me crazy. I wish the men weren't here."

She kissed his neck. "Good. I like driving you nuts. Why should it all be one-sided?"

He nibbled on her lower lip. "I like hearing you say that."

She pulled back enough to see him. "Tell me about your mother."

"You should have seen her after I was shot. As soon as she found out I was going to live, she campaigned for me to practice law instead. She said it was time for me to get out, but I didn't agree with her. Now I'm not so sure. Yesterday when I disarmed the bomb, I wanted to be more than Grayson's arresting officer. I wanted to be the prosecuting attorney who convinced a jury to send the scum up for a long time. I couldn't stand the thought of you getting hurt."

He had so many wonderful qualities, Polly thought. He could be hard as nails or as gentle as a lamb. He could be a tender lover or a demanding one. She'd just scratched the surface of knowing this complex man.

"Thank you," she said. "I couldn't stand to see you hurt either."

A lazy smile replaced the hard frown on his face when he mentioned Grayson's name. Polly's heart skipped a beat.

"When will you phone your mother?" she asked.

"Soon. Polly. I'm sorry. I really am. Hindsight is twenty-twenty vision. I should have come up with another alibi."

Her fingers traced his lips. "We'll get through it."

"Meeting you and making love with you is the only part of this I'm not sorry about."

"Me too," she whispered, meeting his lips for a long kiss. His arms were her refuge. It seemed incongruous she would seek solace in the arms of the man whose sheer audacity had caused her such misery. Yet when they drew apart and started back toward the house, she held on to his hand, as if clinging to an elusive sanctuary.

Activity on and off the bridge hummed with an array of men, trucks, and machinery. One burly, Tshirted man directed the forklift positioning the new planks. There was noise everywhere, men shouting, hammering, sawing, pneumatic drills.

Spotting Jim in the distance, Polly disengaged her hand from Reid's. "We better not."

Reid set his jaw. Just seeing Polly took his breath away, and all he wanted to do was touch her. Her sun-kissed hair, thick and falling in waves below her slim shoulders, made him want to bury his hands in it, as he had when they'd made love. Her cheekbones were high, her skin a creamy rose, the color of the finest porcelain. Her wide blue eyes, surrounded by a lush fringe of lashes, had a slight almond shape to their outer corners, giving her an aristocratic air.

He shoved his hands in his pockets and tried not to think of his impending engagement party. His supposed fiancée was so beautiful, all he wanted to do was grab her by the hand and hustle her into the house, straight up to the bedroom.

As if she'd read his mind, she smiled up at him and whispered, "We'll have time alone later."

"I need a scorecard," he grumbled. "In front of your aunt, touching is not only permissible, it's advisable. After all, Martha sees us producing a passel of babies."

"She is rather amazing."

Reid bit back a smile. "Rather is hardly the word. She believes implicitly in tarot cards, astrological charts, palmistry, and Axl Rose."

"I envy her passion."

Reid stopped in his tracks as he saw the wistful, faraway look in Polly's eyes. "Don't," he said. "She's living in her fantasy world. Unfortunately I helped bring it about. I accept the blame. But as far as you're concerned, Polly, you're the most passionate woman I know."

His lips tightened as he suddenly thought of Polly in the arms of another man. He had no claim on her. What she did in her private life after he left was her business. For himself commitment was merely a word beginning with the letter *C*.

He cleared his throat. "Then," he continued, his hands jammed in his pockets, "there's Jim. He's worked for the police long enough to know that if they pull him off another assignment, this one takes a high priority. Professionally it's a no-no for me to show you affection. You were right to remind me. I'm going to like tomorrow a damn sight better than today. At least kissing you or holding your hand will be expected of me then."

Polly stared up at him as yet another unpleasant thought struck her. Not only would kissing be expected tomorrow, but surely her friends would ask all sorts of questions about her future husband. She didn't know his age, his favorite movies, his favorite ice-cream flavor, or his shirt size. She didn't know his hobbies, what sports he played in high school.

In short, she knew him mainly carnally!

While they pretended to be an adoring couple, none of the groom's side would be in attendance. Unless she counted Fran. Fran and Reid would be the only two people there walking around with concealed weapons. A bubble of hysterical laughter erupted from Polly's throat.

"What's so funny?" Reid asked.

"Funny?" She stared at him, agog. "Funny? Funny!" The word caught on a sob. Tears pooled in her eyes. "I'm laughing to keep from crying, you silly man.

"Can't you see how happy I am? Tomorrow promises to be your everyday garden-variety engagement party. It's every girl's dream. I can't wait."

She broke down sobbing. "Poor Martha."

Reid didn't give a damn if the whole world saw them. All he cared about was not upsetting Polly. He held her while she cried her "tears of happiness."

"I'm sorry," she mumbled. "I don't want you to see me acting like a fool."

"What should I say?" he asked, his lips on her temple.

She didn't answer, and he let her cry it out, turning his body to shield her from prying eyes, should anyone look their way.

The consequences of his actions weighed heavily on his mind. On the one hand they were strangers. On the other hand they craved each other intimately.

They were engaged.

Engaged to be disengaged.

He didn't want to give her up.

He had to give her up.

Swiftly. A clean, surgical break. He should be used to them by now. Circumstances had thrown them together. Circumstances would part them.

When she finally stopped crying, he lifted her face to his with one finger under her chin. He kissed the sheen of tears from her lashes, her cheeks.

"Better?" he asked softly.

She wiped her face. "Yes. Now that I think about it, it won't be so bad. I'll put tomorrow to good use. Writers use their experiences in books. This one will end up a scene in my book. In fact, I'll write down everything that's happened since we met. I'll watch you when you mingle with the crowds, then adapt your actions for my book. So you see, nothing in life is wasted. Consider yourself important to my research."

It wasn't exactly what Reid wanted to hear, but at least she had stopped crying. They continued on to the house, and he tried to call his mother. Her line was busy. He tried several times with no luck, so he decided to make lemonade for the crew. Polly told him where to find paper cups and a few boxes of chocolate-chip cookies on a pantry shelf.

As they carried the lemonade and cookies outside, Jim came to meet them. He'd finished his inspection, and as he'd suspected, the bridge was safe except for one rotted section.

Polly smiled in relief. "Thank goodness! If I had to replace the bridge, it would cost a fortune, which I don't have."

Jim wiped his sweaty brow. "You're getting away lucky too, Polly. New bridges are outrageously expensive. Especially without state aid, and this being private property, I doubt if you'd qualify. The men will support the braces. By leaving the old ones in and drilling new ones, it makes the bridge sturdier. I said it before, Polly, but after seeing a few of those rotted boards, I'm amazed you didn't fall through."

Reid looked down at the rushing river and was grateful for Polly's safety.

"Whoever the guy is you're after," Jim went on, "he might have fallen through and saved you the trouble of setting a trap."

As Reid joined Jim to inspect the repairs on the bridge, Polly returned to the house. Since only a miracle would now prevent half the town from coming to her house the following day, she threw herself into a frenzy of cleaning. She was on her knees, attacking a stubborn spot on the kitchen linoleum, when Reid entered the house about forty-five minutes later.

He paused at the kitchen door. "Do you want some help?"

She shook her head vigorously. "No," she said between gritted teeth. "I'm pretending this damn floor's a punching bag."

He watched her for another minute, then turned to go. "I'll try my mother again."

"Use the phone in my office. When you're through, switch on the answering machine."

The phone had been ringing to distraction. Her closest friends were thrilled, surprised, and, she learned, hurt that she hadn't mentioned Reid. Grace Waters teasingly accused her of holding out on her, but there was a note of disappointment in her voice.

"We're best friends," she complained. "Best friends talk."

Polly apologized. She promised they'd get together for lunch, and she'd tell Grace everything.

After she figured it out first for herself.

Lonni Landis's congratulations ended in a scolding too. "Why didn't you say something? We're best friends. Best friends talk."

Polly promised they'd get together for lunch, when she'd tell her everything. She'd use the same story she would tell Grace.

Joan Daniels said they'd known each other since grade school. She came right out and asked Polly why she'd held out on her.

Polly told Joan what she'd told the others, adding, "I didn't want to jinx our romance."

Lying to her friends pained her. She hoped when she was able to explain, they'd understand. If not, it would strain friendships with people she loved and admired.

She could hear Reid's voice in the den and assumed he'd gotten through to his mother. He returned to the kitchen doorway about five minutes later.

She sat back on her haunches. "How did it go?"

"You're wearing out the same spot."

She hadn't realized. She rose and picked up the mop. "What did your mother say?"

"Everything's fine. When you're through, let's talk."

She flipped her hair back and gave him a level stare. "No. I'm through dissecting the nuances of our sham engagement. We've talked it to death."

"If you need me, I'll be in the barn, setting up the camera."

By afternoon Polly had finished cleaning. She'd scrubbed the kitchen, bathroom, and pantry, and she'd vacuumed. Since Reid still had not returned, she took advantage of his absence to do a little writing. She had barely switched on her computer when she heard his voice.

"Polly."

She turned to see him standing in the doorway. "All through?"

"For now. Polly, we need to talk."

His worried expression alerted her. "The last time you said that, I didn't like the conversation. Am I going to like this one?"

He gazed at her steadily. "I doubt it."

"Then go away. I don't want to hear it."

When he walked into the room and put his hand on her shoulder, she knew the news was bad.

"I started to tell you before," he said, "but you were so upset, I thought I'd wait. Honey, my mother is coming."

His announcement hit her like a hammer, rapping on her chest. Slowly, and with the utmost deliberation, she forced herself to talk. She spoke only one word. "Why?"

"She thinks with your aunt knowing she lives in Pittsburgh, it could raise questions if no one from my family comes."

"But she knows it's a make-believe engagement."

"It's the principle, she said when I reminded her that this is a cover. Furthermore, she's worried that if she doesn't attend, she won't do her bit for our safety. Then there's Martha and you."

"She doesn't know us."

"True, but my mother feels your aunt's friends may think she doesn't approve of you."

Drawing a ragged breath, Polly stood up, her hands clenched into fists. "How can she disapprove of a stand-in fiancée she's never met?"

"It's more than that. If Martha asks you about your future mother-in-law, you won't know what to say since you don't know her. I understand where she's coming from. I wish you would," he said moodily.

As her spirits drooped, Polly's voice rose contentiously. "Reid, I ask myself why life is dumping on me in catastrophic proportions. I can't come up with the answer. Why is it that when I'm around you, one disaster ends and another mushrooms?"

His own temper flaring, he snapped back, "How about remembering who refused to keep her aunt away? Dammit, I'm here to catch Grayson."

"Fine. Everything is my fault! I still don't want to meet your mother! Can't you stop her?"

"No!" he bellowed, stalking around the room like a caged lion. "She's a grown woman. I'm not responsible for her actions. Can you stop your aunt? She's the one making this shindig. Do you think I'm looking forward to it any more than you are?"

"But none of it's real. Call your mother back. Tell her again."

"I already told you she knows, and I've told you why she insists on coming. My mother is covering the bases. I don't agree with her, but I'll be damned if I'll stop her. How will it look when your aunt invites her to her own son's engagement party and she refuses to attend? Not very nice. Besides, she's worried your aunt may be a loose cannon."

"She is not!" Polly cried defensively.

"I know that, and you know that, but how many women name milk cows Horace? Or turn the cow on to Axl Rose's music? Or read your future in your pinkie finger?"

Polly couldn't argue with him when she considered how the scenario sounded to his mother. Frustrated, she threw up her hands. "This is great! In addition to all that, I'm engaged to a man I don't know."

"You know me intimately," he reminded her.

Her mouth dropped open. Even though she was furious with him, she knew he was right. They'd talked a long time after making love the night before, learning more about each other than their bodies, but still not enough to carry her through a multitude of questions. Not the sort of questions her friends would ask. She knew he was so handsome, he could make the most casual clothes look elegant, and she knew how he looked with no clothes on. He was a proud male with warrior instincts and the ability of a masterful lover. A jolt of memory ran through her, and she ran her tongue over her lips.

"What happens tomorrow," she said, "if people ask us things about each other and we don't know the answers?"

"Like what?" he asked.

"Our preferences. Allergies. Hobbies. Favorite colors, movies, actors, TV. Mundane important things that stamp a person as unique. You don't know if I color my hair."

"Do you?"

"No."

"Then why in hell should I have known that?"

"Because," she said ineffectually.

He snorted. "Anyway, I knew it's natural."

"How?"

His gaze traveled downward. "Guess."

She gasped, her cheeks blooming with color. "Get out of my office."

"Not until we have this out." He grabbed a pad and pen from her desk, then lifted her easily and carried her upstairs.

"Put me down!"

"No!"

She pounded his back as he mounted the stairs. She might as well be flicking a fly for all the attention he paid to her.

He strode into her bedroom and dumped her on the bed, then walked back to the door and locked it.

She scrambled to sit up. "You are crazy!"

He planted his legs apart, put his hands on his hips, and glowered at her. "Yes, as a matter of fact, I am. Since meeting you, I have been completely crazy. You're the most irritating female I've ever met. On the other hand you're also the bravest. Regardless, my sweet, we will stay here until we know each other better. Fire away with your questions." He tossed the pen and pad to her. "Write down my answers."

Her temper spiked. "I don't have to do a damn thing. Go to hell. After you leave my room."

He took off his belt. "Not a chance. You said we didn't know the important little things about each other. We're going to talk. And while we talk, we'll strip until we're down to the bare essentials."

"You're mad. Absurd. A lunatic."

"I'm all of that. Take off your clothes."

"I will not. Put your belt on. Fran's liable to walk in any minute."

"She's not coming today."

Polly's eyes narrowed. "How do you know?"

"I called her a few minutes ago. Tom's still in pretty bad shape, and I told her to stay with him. I assured her I had everything under control. If we hear from the surveillance team that Grayson's changed his plans and is coming today or tonight, she can be here before him. If not, she's coming first thing in the morning. By the way, she knows we're 'engaged.'"

"So, Ms. Sweet, we're alone. Before this day ends, there won't be much we don't know about each other. My favorite ice creams are mocha chip and rocky road. What's yours?"

"Vanilla."

His shirt sailed to the dresser. "Vanilla." He shook his head. "No imagination. Are your eyes cornflower blue?"

"So what if they are?"

"Good, then that's my favorite color. See how easy this is? Write that down."

"You're insane."

"We've established that. And remember, we're starting out even. The blouse, Polly. Your hair is the shade of sun-ripened flax. Put that down for my second-favorite color."

"You lied to Fran."

"I'm getting to be an expert at it where you're concerned. I amaze myself. I'm an honest person who lies like a trooper. No pun intended. I wear white underwear. I prefer socks a solid color. Write that down in case your friends ask."

"If you so damned honest," she yelled, "why did you tell Fran to stay away?"

"In this whole ludicrous, cockeyed scam I can't stand the thought of sleeping without you tonight. I'm a man who prefers sleeping alone, so why do I want you in my arms? Maybe it's because you're the most responsive woman I know. Maybe it's preordained. I'll be damned if I know why." He sat in the wing chair to untie his shoes. "But you tell me. Do you like the idea of us sleeping apart tonight?"

She felt her cheeks flame. He was angry for wanting her. What should she say? She lifted her chin.

"If you're waiting for an answer, you won't get one."

One of his shoes hit the floor. "I already know the answer. Either take off your blouse or say good-bye to it. I like chicken soup, split-pea soup, not too thick, and tomato soup. Nothing creamed."

"You're seducing me!"

He smiled grimly. "Wrong. You're seducing me. You have been from the first moment I kissed you. Probably from the first moment you opened your sassy mouth. Fate, in the person of your aunt Martha, brought us together, so don't blame me. I'm carrying out higher orders. Besides, I asked not to come here."

"Are you sorry now?" she asked, her heart hammering so wildly she could hardly think. Suddenly his answer was the most important thing in the world.

His keen gaze grew serious. "What do you think?"

She tried and failed to keep her aplomb. "I . . . I don't know."

"Polly," he said, seeing the slightest trembling to her lower lip. "No, I'm not sorry. That's the one thing I'm clear about."

When a glow of pleasure warmed her eyes, he smiled and reverted to teasing her.

"Why aren't you writing down my words of wisdom? You said the little things are important. In case anyone asks, my favorite late-night talk-show hosts are Jay Leno and Arsenio Hall. I read Tom Clancy and Dean Koontz, among others. It's safe to say I love books. Fiction, nonfiction. When yours is finished, I'd like to read it."

His other shoe hit the floor.

He stood and unfastened his pants. As she stared at him, he dropped them on the floor.

"You can tell your friends," he went on, "that I prefer casual clothes. Jeans and sneakers, when possible. My dress suits are mixed: gray, blue, brown. My dress shoes come in two colors: black and brown. I'm an expert swimmer. I'm not very neat. Don't tell them that. It's too personal."

Polly's eyes widened in appreciation as his briefs landed atop his trousers. It was getting hard for her to think about mundane things with Reid naked. Her fingers itched to touch him, to feel his male beauty inside her. But she sat upright, thoughts of lovemaking evaporating, as he turned and started rummaging through her dresser.

"You're messing up my neat drawers," she exclaimed.

"I'm learning the important things about you. It might come up in conversation."

He flipped through her lingerie, pausing to hold up a shimmering emerald-green teddy accented with black lace. "Wow! I bet you look terrific in this. Later, you'll try it on for me."

Flabbergasted, she watched as he tossed it aside and picked up another. He held up a one-piece animal-print teddy that wrapped around like a diaper. "You're full of delicious surprises."

"Put my lingerie back where you found it. What do you think you're doing?" she demanded.

"Getting ready for tomorrow. You're the one who's worried I might be asked a question I can't answer. This is my crash course." He faced her. "I can tell everyone about your underwear. It's one of the little important things. Right?"

When she only gaped at him, he continued. "If there's a lull in the conversation, be sure to tell your friends I broke my right arm when I was ten. In the summertime. I couldn't swim. It'll raise my sympathy level, especially with women. Write that down."

She didn't, nor would she admit he was making a mockery of her worries, showing her in his unorthodox manner how insignificant they were.

"Cat got your tongue?" he asked. "No matter. I love Chinese food, but I can't master chopsticks. That should go over big. Write that down."

She saw his point. She had stressed the trivial. Maybe tomorrow wouldn't be so bad. Maybe it would be good. Maybe Reid would come back to see her after this was over, and they could date like normal people. Then again, maybe he wouldn't! If he did, they'd have to keep up the pretense of being engaged.

He sat down beside her, his weight indenting the bed. Taking the blank pad and pen from her lap, he set them on the floor. "Where was I?"

Without waiting for an answer, he kissed her fingers, then sucked each one. His tongue found nerves she didn't know she had.

"I see you have writer's cramp. We'll talk instead."

She giggled. "You're stark naked."

He wiggled his feet. "Except for my socks. I can't be entirely naked. I'm courting you." He put his arm around her.

Her heart slammed against her ribs. She hesitated a moment. "This is your idea of courtship?"

He kissed her neck. "What did you think I was doing?"

"Seducing me." She glanced down at his magnificent form. "With your socks on."

He lifted one foot. "You object to my socks? Or is it the color?"

"Most men send flowers."

He snuggled closer. "I'm speeding the process. However, I'm going to feel like the worst kind of damned fool if I stripped for nothing."

The tension over the party slipped from her shoulders as another kind of tension took its place. She felt hot and cold. A shiver ran through her as she remembered his skill as a lover. Arousal made her shakier than she'd been when he'd mentioned courtship.

With one hand he flung her hair back over her shoulder, then he trailed kisses from her neck to the valley between her breasts.

"You're slow, Polly. I'll help you." He unbuttoned her blouse, then slid it over her shoulders. As if he were a magician, it and her bra sailed onto the floor. Her shorts went next.

He kissed her bikinis off, sending her wild.

"Who's your favorite actor?" he asked. "Aside from old Leslie Howard. Anyone from this century?"

He was sucking her breasts, moving from one to the other and driving her mad. She gasped out a name. He wasn't listening, though. He flicked his tongue against her nipple, and she moaned, rubbing herself against him. His hand slid down her body to between her legs, and she arched against it.

He lifted his head, his eyes searing hers. "Talk to me," he whispered.

"My favorite color is . . ."

He kissed her lips, then trailed a hot path down her neck to her breasts. He came back to murmur against her mouth. "Tell me what's important. What were you saying about colors?"

She tugged his hair. "I don't know. Whatever I happen to like at the moment. Not brown. It makes me sallow."

He blew in her ear. "You?" He chuckled. "You couldn't look sallow if you tried. In your romance book what happens to the hero?"

She licked his lips. "His life is changed forever."

He kissed her stomach. "Mmmm. You taste delicious. What about the heroine's life?"

"Who?" she asked, sinking into a sensual haze.

Reid positioned himself between her legs. "The heroine."

"Who cares?"

"I do. Talk to me, sweetheart."

He slipped inside her. At the first stroke her eyes flew open. "In a romance you can't have the hero and heroine riding off into the sunset in opposite directions."

"What about real life? Will the romance novelist listen to her heart and let nature take its course?" he asked, trapping her with words as surely as with his body.

Her muscles tightened around him, giving him her answer.

Many hours later, long after the bridge repairs were finished and they'd said goodbye to Jim, Reid and Polly spent a quiet evening curled up on the couch.

Reid's hand drifted to her breast, and she snuggled closer. His mind wasn't on the movie showing on TV. It was on Polly. It had happened again. Each time he made love to her, it got better. Hotter. Spiraling out of control. Which made it worse. Dangerous. Combustible.

His gun lay on the floor in its holster. He couldn't tell her why the word "courtship" had slipped out. His life was taking a strange and powerful turn, thanks to his having met this one brave, beautiful, glorious woman.

Polly spelled the *C* word.

Commitment.

TEN

Unable to stop the clock, Polly and Reid got out of bed the following morning with more than a little reluctance. Polly looked out the window. The sky was a blast of blue, perfect for a blast of a party. Leaving Reid, she went to the barn, milked Horace, then returned to bathe and dress in shorts and a top. For the party she would wear the animal-print teddy—for Reid—but she couldn't decide which dress to wear. She wanted to look her best. She and Reid would be judged that day by a jury of her peers.

The first peer who judged her was herself.

She was in love with Reid. A complicating but true fact. He said he loved seeing the radiance light up her eyes. He said he loved making love to her. He hadn't said, "I love you."

She loved everything about him, even if she didn't know all there was to know about the nonconformist who'd stolen her heart.

She knew the essentials, though. He was a man of character. He wouldn't purposely hurt anyone. He had a sense of humor. He was intelligent and kind. In reality, she was the one who had gotten them into this mess. She had insisted on her aunt having access to her home, and he had gone along with her, coming up with what seemed to be the best solution. She had never considered the additional strain she placed on Reid. He hadn't wanted the engagement party, nor did he look forward to his mother's arrival.

In effect, he was caught in a juggling act, trying to calm her and put a good face on a bad bargain. There was no doubt he was attracted to her, but only wishful thinking and the wildest stretch of her imagination would mistake infatuation for love.

He'd used the term "courtship" in the heat of the moment. He had no intention of leaving the force, settling down in a big old house, marrying her, and fulfilling Martha's prediction.

At least he had taught her a valuable lesson: Don't sweat the small stuff. Concentrate on what's important. Character counted, not the mundane unimportant things one learns over time.

Provided one had the time. They didn't. His primary purpose was to apprehend Grayson. In a day or two he'd be gone.

Fran had arrived while she was in the shower. Polly was brushing her hair when Fran came into her bedroom, carrying two mugs of coffee. Reid, thankfully, had made the bed and removed all traces of himself from the room while Polly had been milking Horace.

"Hi," Fran said. "Reid sent this for you." She handed Polly one of the mugs.

"How's Tom?" Polly asked.

"He's fine. I fussed over him sufficiently and left him with a pot of chicken soup. It's good for everything. Not necessarily for the patient, but for the nervous friend who has to be doing something."

Polly understood completely. Picturing Reid in the line of duty could easily send her to cooking for an army.

"What does Tom do?" Polly asked.

"He owns a toy store. We met when I asked him for suggestions for toys for my three-year-old niece. She and I had made out a list, but after one look at Tom, the list stayed in my purse. He took my breath away."

Fran sipped her coffee, winking at Polly over the rim of the mug. "He still does."

"How does he feel about your profession?" Polly asked as she chose several outfits from her closet and laid them on the bed.

"I'm sure he wishes I were doing something else, but this is what I chose. He knew that when we met. It didn't stop us from falling in love or planning a wedding. We want children too. If I change my mind about working in the field, I'll ask for reassignment. There's lots I can do inside."

"Do you see yourself doing that?" Polly set a chartreuse linen-blend sheath next to a floral dress. "Which do you prefer?"

Fran cocked her head, looking first at Polly, then at the two outfits. "Wear the flowery dress. It's romantic, perfect for a garden party."

Polly agreed. Made of cotton with a print of roses on a white background, the dress had a fitted bodice, gently scooped neckline, and full, flirty skirt.

"In answer to your question," Fran went on, "if I ask for a desk job, it won't be easy. I'm like Reid. We relish excitement, the charge of adrenaline. He may be tiring of it, though. He plans to practice law. I thought he might make the jump after he was shot. Yet here we both are, still arresting the bad guys."

She turned to leave and paused at the door. "Polly, I know today will be hard for you. Reid told me about your aunt Martha, why you're both going through with this. I think it's noble of you not to want to hurt her feelings. But your aunt's predictions aside, any woman who tries to change Reid is the wrong woman for him. If it's meant to be, he'll come around on his own."

Message received, Polly thought. Having decided on her attire, she hung the clothes back in the closet and went downstairs. Reid was on his way out the front door, and he told her some men from the department had arrived to set up more surveillance equipment in the barn. She watched out the screen door as he and Fran joined three men beside a plain gray van parked in the driveway, then all of them started walking toward the barn.

While she had the house to herself, Polly began making ice, emptying the ice trays into plastic bags, and refilling the trays with water. She cut flowers from her garden for the kitchen and dining-room tables, then she escaped into her den. To her surprise she was able to forget everything but the story. When Reid knocked on her door some time later, she was amazed that two hours had passed.

"All done," he said. "Everyone is ready. The guys rigged lights that operate on sensors, plus recording equipment."

He smiled and pulled her out of her chair, wrapping her in his arms.

"Be careful," she warned, though she was unable to resist him or the quickening of her pulse. "The door's open. Fran will see us."

"She's in the other room. Besides, she knows we're more than casual acquaintances."

Polly's stomach dropped. Fran had issued her friendly warning for a reason.

"How can she suspect anything?"

He framed her face in his large hands. "Polly, she's my partner. It's bad enough to pretend with strangers or your aunt and my mother, but there's no way I'm going to jam my hands in my pockets when it's just Fran. It's hard to be near you and not want to touch you."

She felt herself blush as she remembered all the

touching they'd done the night before. To his delight she'd taken the lead and had made love to him with complete abandon. Looking up at him, she saw he was remembering, too, but then his expression became serious, professional.

"Tomorrow," he said, "I want you to spend the day at your aunt's. If necessary, you'll sleep there. Tell Martha your plumbing's not working. Tell her anything, but I don't want you here."

"Grayson's one man. You said you'll have other police here. Since he left the jewels in the barn, he'll return there for them. I'm perfectly safe in my home."

"Don't argue with me on this," he said firmly. "There's been a change of plans. Grayson isn't coming alone. We picked up a conversation between other members of the gang. They suspect him of skimming jewelry for himself. On his last robbery he didn't deliver as much merchandise as they'd expected."

"If they didn't do the actual stealing, how would they know?"

"From others who'd cased the store beforehand. The network of thieves spying on thieves is long and deep. It's a question of Big Brother watching over your shoulder, in this case, Grayson's. If it's true, and if the mob is on to him, they won't let him out of their sight. When he comes, he'll have company. Of course, that's good news for us. It saves us the trouble of rounding these guys up on our own."

Cold reality washed over her. A few hours ago they'd been making love, oblivious to everything but each other. Now he was saying he'd be putting his life on the line again. She found it hard to swallow.

Instinctively she clutched his arms, ready to beg him not to be part of it. Then she relaxed her hold. She wouldn't add to his worries. Priorities, he'd said. Concentrate on what's important.

She bit her lip hard. "All right. But I'll have to make arrangements for Horace." She thought a moment. "Craig Bucher lives down the road. You'll meet him today. He owns cows. I'm sure he won't mind caring for Horace."

Reid nodded. "Okay, but don't ask him at the party. People will be using the bathrooms this afternoon. They'll know the plumbing works."

"I'll call him an hour or so after he goes home."

"That's my girl."

She knew it was a figure of speech, but she wished it weren't. She wished he'd meant it. She wished it with all her heart.

Making a big production of looking at her watch, she gasped and said it was time for her to get ready. She raced past him and up the stairs. Half an hour later, as she was applying her last touches of makeup, he knocked on the door. When she called for him to come in, he opened the door and stepped inside the room. Her eyes widened in appreciation when she saw that he had changed too. He was wearing a blue linen blazer, off-white linen slacks, and a matching shirt, open at the neck. He might prefer casual clothes, she thought, but he looked dynamite in more formal ones.

"Everything okay?" he asked.

"Everything's fine."

She stood up, and his glance slid to her left hand. "Don't forget the engagement ring. Where is it?"

Her stomach turned over. The fabulous diamond set in platinum signified nothing. She'd be thrilled if Reid put a diamond chip on her finger.

"It's on the dresser."

He picked it up and handed it to her. "Here." Apparently seeing the reluctance on her face, he added, "It's part of the act, Polly. It's just for today."

She slipped it on her finger. "When do you expect your mother?"

"She's here. So's Martha. I left the two of them downstairs." He squeezed her hand. "Don't worry. She'll think you're as lovely as I do."

Thinking he meant the dress, she pirouetted. "Fran likes it too."

"I meant you, not the dress," he said gently.

Awash with emotion, she touched her lips to his.

"All right," she said as she stepped back. "I'm ready to meet your mother."

"I'm not." Cupping her face, he placed his mouth over hers. "This," he said an eternity later, "is no pretense. It's real."

Reid let her precede him from the room. He stole a parting glance at the canopied bed, then followed her downstairs. Hearing voices, they went to the screened-in porch, where they found his mother on her knees inspecting the Victorian wicker rocker. Martha sat on a chair near her. The women were jabbering like old friends. The sight made him smile.

"Mom, you never could resist damaged wicker."

Betty Cameron's head swung around. "You caught me!" she said. She got up as easily as a twenty-year-old, and he introduced her to Polly. Betty Cameron was a stylishly dressed auburn-haired woman with lively green eyes. She wore a green-and-white rayon challis dress with a single strand of pearls.

Betty held on to Polly's hand. "You're the young lady who saved my son from falling into the river. I'm forever in your debt."

Polly and Reid exchanged startled looks. "How did you know?" Reid asked.

"I told her," Martha said as she stood. She looked like a flame in a bright red silk dress, a gold belt, gold bangle bracelets, and red enamel drop earrings.

"How did *you* know?" Polly asked, astounded.

"That nice man, Jim, told me when I brought the men drinks and cookies. Jim said you beat me to it, Reid, and we got to talking."

Reid saw his elaborate cover ruined. "You were supposed to stay off the bridge."

"I know, but after I saw you and Polly walking on it, I figured it was okay for me too. I was being neighborly."

He gritted his teeth. Jim hadn't mentioned Martha when they had spoken again. Now Polly was sending him a silent warning not to hurt her aunt's feelings. In shock he saw his mother's lips purse in warning too.

"That was a nice thing to do," he said to Martha. "What else did you and Jim talk about?"

Martha tapped a pink-frosted fingernail on her chin, her face a study in concentration. Reid held his breath.

"He's married. His wife's name is Alice. They have two children. I told him I read palms. I read his. His pinkie too. Poor man. Two children are his limit."

Reid blanched. Polly gripped the side of a chair. Betty Cameron smiled beatifically.

"Isn't that nice?" Betty said. "I've always wanted to be a grandmother. In the usual order, of course. Marriage, then children."

Martha agreed. "I didn't tell Jim about your twins, Reid, or the son and daughter who follow the twins."

"That was very considerate of you, Aunt Martha. Please don't tell anyone about your predictions."

Polly couldn't meet Reid's gaze. What must his mother think of her and her aunt? She didn't need a mirror to know her face was crimson.

Reid took her elbow, forcing her to look at him. His smile warmed her heart. He was telling her to leave it to him, and she would. Gladly.

"Honey," he said, "my mother would love a tour

of your charming house. Aunt Martha, why don't you and I go outside and direct the workmen where to set up?"

Without waiting, he swooped Martha up. Her feet skimmed the floor as Reid whisked her from the room. Her voice floated behind her as she called Reid a naughty boy. She sounded as if she loved every minute of his attention.

Betty was laughing. "She's an original."

"Martha has a heart of gold. I love her," Polly said, letting Reid's mother know she wouldn't allow her to speak unkindly of Martha.

"I meant," Betty said gently, "that I think she's charming. She's fortunate to have you for a defender, but I don't think she needs one. When I said she's an original, it was with the greatest respect."

Flustered, Polly sought to make amends, but Betty shook her head.

"I'd think less of you if you didn't defend her. It says a lot about your character. Your aunt is a very bright woman. We had a long talk. She's convinced Reid loves you."

Polly's cheeks flamed again. "Please don't take her seriously. Naturally she'd speak freely with you. She thinks our engagement is real. We'll get through today, and by Wednesday Reid will be gone. In no time he'll have forgotten his enforced engagement party." Her voice caught. "It may provide him a few laughs in the future."

Betty reached for her hand. "I seriously doubt that. I saw the way my son looked at you."

Not sure what to say, Polly turned and led Betty into the kitchen. The older woman ran her hand along the highly polished tabletop. "Your father was a talented man. I'm eager to see his paintings. You have your own talents as well. Reid mentioned that you made that needlepoint cushion on the window seat, that you're a teacher, and that you're writing a romance novel."

"He's told you a lot about me," Polly blurted out in surprise.

"Not the little unimportant things. He's obviously proud of you."

Polly ducked her head so Betty couldn't see the sheen of tears in her eyes. "Is he?" she asked, her voice choked.

"Yes. He made sure I know of your talents. Why do you suppose he wanted me to know?"

"I haven't the faintest idea," Polly murmured. Her mind was racing with possibilities, none of which amounted to much. Maybe to put his mother in an agreeable frame of mind, help her get through the day.

"May I sit?" Betty asked.

"Please."

"Has Reid told you how his father proposed to me?"

Polly wet her lips. She had no idea why the conversation was taking such a highly personal turn, nor why Reid would tell her that story. "No."

"Reid's father was tall and impressive, like his son. When Brad and I met on a blind date, the last thing on his mind was marriage. He slipped that in on the phone. I told him I agreed with him. At my age I wanted to do things, see the world, make a career for myself. Marriage and babies weren't on my mind. After we set the date, I learned that he was on the rebound. He had been engaged to a girl, but she had broken it off some months earlier. I asked my sister to call him back and cancel the date, to say I'd broken my leg."

Polly leaned forward. "What happened?"

Betty laughed. "Fate. My sister said not only wasn't there anything wrong with my leg, there was nothing wrong with my mouth! If I wanted to cancel the date, I should do my own dirty work.

"I chickened out and kept the date. When Brad picked me up, we took one look at each other and laughed from relief. That night Brad announced he intended to marry me. He never asked."

"What did you say?" Polly asked, intrigued.

Betty smiled impishly. "I told him he was crazy. Then he kissed me. If he was crazy, then so was I. I found heaven in his arms. We were married a month later. Our lives were gloriously intertwined until Brad's death two years ago." Betty sent Polly a meaningful look. "Reid takes after his father."

Polly swallowed.

Betty took her hand. "Did you think my only reason for coming here was to support Reid's alibi?"

"Wasn't it?"

"No. I wanted to meet the woman who would cause him to concoct such a ludicrous excuse. You must have gotten under his skin fast. When I asked him who'd thought of the idea to say you two were engaged, he admitted he did. Were you surprised?"

"Shocked. When we first met, I couldn't stand him. I let him know it too."

Betty grinned, her smile so like Reid's. "What happened to change your mind?"

We kissed and I found heaven in his arms.

"He's very persuasive."

"But not that persuasive." Betty laughed merrily. "No, I think whatever is transpiring between you must be rattling the cosmos. Martha told me that."

Betty gazed intently at her. "It's interesting that each of you saved the other's life. What do you make of that?"

"If this were a plot problem," Polly said, "it would be simple to manipulate a happy ending. Issues in real life, though, aren't easily tied up in neat bows. Reid's career is law enforcement. It's not living in a small town practicing law and having four children, a milk cow named Horace, and a dog named Cuddles. It lacks excitement."

Betty stood, smoothing the folds of her dress.

"There are all kinds of excitement. Some last far longer than others. Now I'll take the tour of the house, please."

They were just leaving the kitchen when Reid walked in the back door. "Martha's in her glory," he said, chuckling. "After telling the men from the rental company where she wanted everything set up, she brought out Horace's tape recorder. She figured the men should have some music to work to."

"Oh, no!" Polly said, a giggle escaping her.

Reid hugged her, his eyes glinting with amusement. "Yup. I never saw men move so fast. They carted tables, set up umbrellas and chairs, and were long gone before the tape ended."

As she relished Reid's embrace, Polly realized he wasn't hiding his feelings before his mother. He'd hugged her as naturally as if they were alone. She caught his mother's eye. Betty was smiling.

Looking up at Reid, Polly felt her heart fill to overflowing. There was strength and steel and determination in him. There was also softness and empathy and consideration. She very nearly blurted out that she loved this man whose slick, hard body turned her nights into sheer wonder, and whose tenderness had touched her very soul.

The festivities started at one with streams of cars driving across the now-safe bridge. The lawn was a sea of brightly colored tablecloths and umbrellas. Long serving tables displayed a smorgasbord of delicious foods. Desserts with whipped cream crammed Polly's refrigerator. Guests gathered everywhere across the lawn in ever-changing groups.

Polly needn't have worried about Reid's mother. Betty charmed her principal, his wife, and everyone she met, including Polly's closest chums, Grace, Joan, and Lonni. As if born to the plot, Betty, and Fran as well, did their parts. When a comment was called for, Betty said she was delighted Reid had fallen in love with Polly. Fran said she was a longtime friend of Reid's family, and was now a friend of Polly's too.

For their parts Grace, Lonni, and Joan basked in Reid's sunny warmth, his teasing smile. He poured on the charm, always keeping Polly at his side. When he hugged her or kissed her—which he managed to do often—it elicited smiles of approval.

"He's a darn sight better-looking than Ashley Wilkes," Grace murmured to Polly. Smiling at Reid, she suggested that he and Polly and herself and her husband should have dinner together sometime. There was a great Chinese restaurant in town, she added.

Reid winked at Polly, then asked Grace if she knew how to use chopsticks. She said she did. He replied he'd never mastered the art. Polly, who already knew about the chopsticks and could recall vividly the setting of that absurd conversation with Reid, nearly choked on her iced tea.

Reid clapped her on the back. "Wrong pipe, darling?" he asked solicitously.

She swallowed, corralled the first man she saw, and introduced Reid. "He broke his arm when he was ten, isn't that a shame, John? In the summertime too."

"Women," Reid said to John. "You never know what they'll say when they're in love."

John nodded, as if in perfect agreement.

Polly took Reid's arm and walked him on to the next group of guests. Among them was Municipal Court judge Fred Joyce, and she could feel Reid stiffen as she introduced them, as if he were moving into high alert.

"Martha tells me you're an attorney," the judge said.

He asked Reid where he'd gone to law school, and was impressed when he heard Washington University. Joining the conversation, Betty volunteered the information that Reid had graduated third in his class. The judge congratulated Reid, then asked him about some of his teachers, whom the judge knew.

As they spoke, several other attorneys came over to them. All handed Reid their cards and told him to phone. The judge said he'd like to lunch with him. "We'll talk about the town," he added.

As soon as was polite, Reid eased away from the group, taking Polly with him. She walked to the far side of the lawn with him, to where a split-rail fence separated the grazing land from the road.

"What's wrong?" she asked. "Everything is going well."

He shook his head. "My mother goofed. I wish she hadn't talked about me to the judge. She knows I'm not staying here. If I didn't know better, I'd think she was in cahoots with your aunt."

Polly's heart plopped. She felt wretched. Leaning on the fence, she stared out at Horace grazing in the pasture. She had let herself hope Reid would say something about a future. Their future. He obviously never intended to. She'd let her heart chase a fantasy.

Reid remained focused on his goal. To keep Martha out of his hair so he could do his job. And leave. The searing passion they had shared could never compete with his mission. She had served her purpose. She was his weekend in the country.

She turned and walked rapidly toward the barn. If she didn't get away from him, he'd see her cry. She wouldn't give him the satisfaction. She was enough of an idiot as it was, letting his mother lull her with stories. For all she knew, Betty had told them to ensure Polly's sterling performance.

She heard footsteps crunching gravel behind her, then Reid grabbed her arm and spun her around. "Where do you think you're going?"

She gave him a scathing look. "Take your hands off me, or I'll fling this ring in your face."

"For the love of heaven!" he thundered, an instant wariness about him. "What's with you?"

"Nothing. I'm tired of this farce. Poor Judge Joyce was trying to be nice while you gave your mother dagger looks. It's a wonder he didn't see them. Is it okay with you that I prefer to be alone?"

"No, dammit, it's not. You'll ruin everything. If you don't care for your welfare or your aunt's or mine, think of Fran's."

"Why did you ask me to pretend we're lovers? Pretend we're engaged? Surely you could have dreamed up another reason."

"Not at the moment!" he snapped.

She poked his chest. "I'll tell you why, you big, brave macho man! It fed your ego. And in the bargain, you got me."

"If that's what you think, you know nothing about me."

"Bingo!" She heard her voice rise in hysteria. "Now you see my point. I don't know enough. Your mother thinks the sun rises and sets over your head. Martha's bamboozled. I was too. You're good, Reid. If you need a reference, I'll vouch for you as a lover. But one weekend of you is all I can take."

He stiffened. "Then we're both lucky I'm leaving. Isn't that right?"

"You bet we are. I can't wait for this stupid, idiotic afternoon to end."

She heard his teeth grating. He shoved his blazer back and jammed his hands in his pockets.

"Do you intend to come back to the party with me, or is it your intention to blow my cover?"

She looked into his angry face. How could she love

him and deny his safety? She wanted nothing more than to melt in his arms and beg him to take care.

"I'll keep my bargain," she said curtly. "But don't you dare touch me."

Something like pain flashed in his eyes. His mouth grim, he buttoned his blazer and nodded. "Tomorrow you go to your aunt's. I'll let you know when it's safe for you to return."

Miserable, she returned to the party. They mingled. They spoke. They laughed. They accepted plates of food and sat down to eat. He gathered up their empty plates. She poured his drink. They smiled. They did all the things expected of a newly engaged couple madly in love with each other.

Except for one thing.

Not once did they touch.

As hostess, Polly saw to everyone's comfort. She made certain all had plenty to eat and drink. With each wish for a happy and prosperous future, she pasted a smile on her face and thanked the person. By eight that evening the last of the stragglers departed amid a string of good wishes. To Polly, her face frozen in a smile, it seemed an endless parade as she stood at Reid's side, shaking hands, bussing cheeks, promising to phone friends to firm up dates to get together.

"Reid," Martha said later as they were cleaning up the kitchen, "wasn't it nice of Judge Joyce to take you under his wing?"

"Very," he said, watching Polly.

Martha, her face aglow, her bangle bracelets offering a punctuation to her fluttering hands, praised him on the fine impression he made.

He listened as long as he could stand it. After thanking Martha for the wonderful party, he left.

Polly, citing a headache, excused herself shortly afterward. In search of aspirin, she fled upstairs to the bathroom. She took two tablets, then twisted the engagement ring off and marched into Reid's bedroom, leaving it atop his dresser.

She bumped into him as she left the room.

"Polly."

The moment was awkward. His hands reached for her automatically. Despite her heart hammering in her chest, she coolly said, "I returned the ring."

There was awareness in his gaze, as if he was measuring her underlying meaning. "Stay, please. I want to talk to you, explain about this afternoon."

She looked him in the eye. "You needn't trouble yourself. I hadn't realized how difficult it would be for you. We both couldn't wait for it to end. Thank goodness, it has."

"Your aunt was in her glory today. She's still on a high."

"Your mother wasn't doing too badly herself." Because that had sounded mean in her own ears, she added, "I like her. She's a nice woman."

"She likes you too."

"I've got a headache. Good night, Reid."

To her surprise he blocked her path. She'd have thought he'd be only too glad to shed the pretense. She started to brush past him but found herself locked by a strong arm propelling her into his bedroom. Before she could protest, his mouth was covering hers, and he was kissing her deeply. His hands swept down her spine, crushing her close. She tried to pull away. Afraid to make any noise that the others might hear, she was locked in a silent battle for supremacy.

He lifted her and kissed her sensitive neck, then pressed his lips to the underside of her jaw. "Don't shut me out," he said roughly.

She twisted from his grasp before her traitorous body sought the one man it couldn't resist. She kept her arms at her sides, lest she slip them around his neck, or delve her fingers into his hair. She needed no more aching memories to quell, no more reminders that his arousal signified lust while hers meant love.

"Go away," she said.

"Not until you hear me out. I think we should remain engaged for a few weeks. . . ."

ELEVEN

Had Reid suddenly declared his undying love for her, Polly couldn't have been more surprised. Or more hurt. She closed her eyes, fighting for control, then snapped them open.

"May I ask what scheme you've concocted now that has prompted your impetuous desire to continue a counterfeit engagement?"

"You heard Martha. You saw how happy she is. Why douse her happiness? She's old. It's unfair for us to swing her emotions like a pendulum."

Polly didn't bother to hide her fury. She was wounded. Deeply. He wanted a few more weeks of enjoyment with her and was using her aunt as an excuse. He couldn't even be honest about it.

"I'm flattered as hell that you're concerned for my aunt. Since I'm younger, I guess it's okay to swing my emotions. Is that it? You stick around for a few weeks, then you drive off into the sunset. Permanently. On your next case, if your luck keeps up, another woman will succumb to your charms as quickly as I did. You win, I lose. No thanks."

"That's a cheap shot," he retorted, reacting swiftly and angrily, his fierce expression revealing his irritation. "Making love to you was the only time I've mixed business with pleasure."

It took her a moment to grasp his meaning. "I'm glad I measured up to your standards," she said, deaf to his explanation. When he tried to touch her, she shook him off with a quick wave of her hand. "All of which is beside the point. I'll do what I think is right. I'm a practical person. Usually. I'm orderly, not given to . . ."

"To what?" Reid asked gently, seeing her wounded eyes.

She drew herself up straight. "The next time I allow myself to become involved with a man, I won't let emotions rule my behavior."

"Hear me out first," he cajoled. She should know that emotions spurred the practical, the orderly, especially when two people became involved. "I never intended for you to face Martha alone."

He still didn't get it, Polly thought. He had no idea the hurt he'd caused her by saying his mother was in cahoots with Martha. She crossed to the window and stared outside at the lawn that had held the garden party. Floodlights shone on the grass. A breeze picked up a deflated congratulatory balloon and skirted it across the lawn.

Her arms wrapped around her waist, she asked, "What did you intend? To substitute an identical engagement ring for me to wear until you think my aunt's ready for a major disappointment? Forget it. I'm telling her the truth. She'll adjust. She's lived a long time, it won't be her first disappointment."

He stood behind her, not touching her. "Polly, I'm trying to make this right."

She was dying by degrees, even as she was resolved to find the strength to make her position clear. Her senses, however, were almost overwhelmed by his nearness. "Are you? Let me help you out. Don't concern yourself about us. Martha is a wise woman. She knows as I do that love is more than the heat of the moment. It's a commitment for the good times and the bad. It's meeting your partner halfway, often more than halfway. It's building a life anchored on trust and respect. On common goals. When I fall in love, it will be with a man who loves me too. A sham engagement to capture crooks is not my idea of a dream come true. One day maybe Martha's predictions will come to pass."

She drew herself up tall and turned to face him. "Once Martha learns why I agreed to this deception, she'll understand and forgive me. Because she was kept in the dark, her guests will pardon her. I hope they'll understand my decision in keeping silent. Your conscience is absolved, Reid. No one's hurt. You've had an interesting experience. You'll earn another medal. Fran said you've earned many."

As Reid stared down at her for an endless moment, Polly hugged herself to keep from splintering apart. "Are you through?" he asked.

"Yes."

"Good, because I'm not." His hands went to her shoulders, his dark gaze riveted to her face. "Stop talking drivel. I can't give you up."

Her heart plummeted another notch. "So we come to the truth. This isn't about Martha. It's about you. We're terrific in bed, so why end it? I've got a news flash for you. I'm not yours to give up. I'm mine to share if I desire."

"What is it you want from me?" he asked forcefully.

"A permanent breather. Beginning now. An end to this charade. You accused your mother of being in cahoots with my aunt. Cahoots! As if my harmless aunt and your mother, who hadn't met her before today, had mapped out a campaign to trap you."

"That's not why I said it!" he shouted.

"Lower your voice! I don't want them up here."

"I'll shout to the rafters if I want to. I was worried that too many people would know too much about me too soon. When you work undercover, the last thing you want is publicity."

"So go away!" she said, making the hardest speech of her life. "If we're seen together, you'll get plenty of publicity. I can't abide this subterfuge and refuse to put myself through any more unnecessary stress. I insist on having my life back the way it was before I met you. There's no room for discussion."

Reid was stopped by the finality he read in her beautiful eyes, and he knew a hurt sharper than the shock of a bullet. "Tell me one thing. Are you sorry we made love?"

She exhaled on a long sigh. "I'm not that good an actress. But it's past. Over. Until you catch Grayson and the others, you'll be in my prayers. I hope it goes well for you and your team. By the way, I phoned my neighbor. He'll take Horace in the morning. But don't come for me when it's all over. I won't be at my aunt's."

He inhaled sharply. "Where will you go?"

"I've earned a few days for myself. When I return, I'll explain everything to Martha. Good-bye, Reid. Good luck."

Reid watched her leave. It was as if she had taken the sun's rays with her, leaving him to grope in a dark tunnel. All day he'd watched each word he uttered. He'd played the intended groom, grateful for Polly at his side as they spoke with her many friends. But when the attorneys and Judge Joyce had accepted him as one of their own, he'd been on his own. And he'd handled it badly. He couldn't blame Polly for being angry with him.

If he declared his true feelings, though, she would think him nuts. After all her talk about how long it took for people to know one another, he didn't dare say he loved her. How could he have fallen in love this fast?

This deeply? If he found it overwhelming, and if he questioned it, then Polly, with her practical sense for the orderly, would think it another one of his ruses to continue an affair.

From the top of the stairs he heard Martha discussing catering halls with Fran and his mother. Little wonder Polly had fled from them. For the first time in his life he envied Ashley Wilkes. If he were Ashley Wilkes, Polly would be running toward him instead of away from him.

Polly was ready to leave early the following morning, the same as Betty. She put Cuddles in the car, then hugged Fran.

"I've written down where I'll be. Call me after you've arrested Grayson. Let me know how you are." She pressed the slip of paper into Fran's hand.

"Shouldn't you give this to Reid?" Fran asked, pocketing the paper.

Polly glanced to where Reid was speaking to his mother. "No, we've already said good-bye." She got in her car. "Let him know there's a lemon-meringue pie in the refrigerator. He told me it's his favorite. Help yourselves to anything else you'd like. There's food for an army. And when you go, leave the house keys in the planter near the front door."

Fran thanked her and said good-bye, and Polly turned her attention to Cuddles, who was in his dog carrier. She had phoned her aunt earlier, saying she needed to do research for her book and would be gone for two days, that Horace was at their neighbors, and she was taking Cuddles. Martha had assumed Reid was leaving too.

After assuring herself Cuddles would survive the short drive, she straightened in her seat. Reid was standing beside her door, one hand on the roof of the car. She let herself drink in the sight of him, caught up in a swirling tide of familiar emotion, wishing she could put her arms around him and feel the magic of him inside of her again. She had spent a restless night, missing him. But he didn't need her for more than sex, not the way she needed him.

He reached in the open window, and his knuckles briefly touched her cheek. "Take care of yourself, Polly. Cuddles, be good to her."

"Reid . . ."

"Yes?"

Her heart thrummed. She bit her bottom lip. "Take care. Don't be a dead hero."

His hand tapped the car roof. He nodded, then stepped back. She could swear she felt his potent male power recede like the tides.

She turned on the ignition and put the car in gear. How shallow her parting words sounded. Twice they had faced danger. From her rearview mirror she saw Reid and Fran talking. Both wore guns. As she turned onto the county road, a van passed over and crossed over her bridge. She knew it contained police personnel. The waiting game had started in earnest.

＊———————＊

Reprimanding herself for her rotten timing, for the way she'd spoken to Reid right before he faced more danger, Polly died a thousand deaths in the motel room. Afraid to leave and miss Fran's call, she resisted the temptation to drive home and stay with her aunt. But she hadn't expected distance would magnify her worry.

"Cuddles, you miss him, too, don't you?"

The dog cocked his head, as if trying to understand the reason for his mistress's sad voice. As the sun went down on the longest day of her life, she tossed the pad of lined paper back into her overnight case. Attempting to write had proved futile. She tried reading and then watching TV, but she couldn't concentrate. Food was no problem. She couldn't eat. She imagined Grayson and whoever else was with him, their guns drawn, shooting it out with the police. She spent the night bouncing from the bed to the bathroom.

Worried she might not hear the phone if it rang, she didn't shower all day Tuesday. By late that night she was ready to climb the walls. Cuddles, who missed Horace, their playful routine, and his padded wicker bed, fussed and whined. She piled towels on the floor for him, but without the cozy sides of his basket, he hated it. Finally she picked him up and held him in her arms until the exhausted dog fell asleep.

She kept an eye on the digital clock and imagined all sorts of horrible scenarios. Why hadn't she told Reid she loved him? Why had she been so stubborn? In time he might have fallen in love with her too. Instead she'd paraded him before strangers, ignoring the fact that he was on duty and didn't want people knowing too much about him.

At midnight the phone rang. She knocked over the lamp in her lunge for the phone, grabbing the receiver on the first ring.

"It's over, Polly," Fran said. "We got them. The whole lousy bunch of thieves." She sounded excited. "For a while we worried Grayson changed his plans. He was riding in the car with the head of the ring, only our guys lost them." She bubbled on, but Polly only wanted to hear if Reid was all right.

"Fran!" she cut in more sharply than she intended. "Is everyone safe?"

"Polly, I'm sorry," Fran said, obviously aware of who Polly meant. "Reid's fine. He was marvelous. He tricked them."

Polly heaved a sigh of relief. He was safe. That was all that mattered.

Fran was laughing so hard, she could barely talk. "After you left, Reid rigged up Horace's tape recorder to blast out a Guns N' Roses tape when he pressed a control attached to a lead wire. We knew when the crooks were in the loft defusing what they thought was a bomb. Reid turned the tape on at the perfect moment." She laughed again. "We got it on video. You should have seen them all jump. They thought they were being blown to bits accompanied by Guns N' Roses. Hang on a minute."

Polly heard voices in the background, then Fran was back on the line. "The press is here taking down the story."

"How do they know?"

"Police reporters file stories from headquarters. Besides, they know most everything that's going on. News crews descended here like locusts. It's going out on all the wires how Reid tricked those dopes. Catch it on the news tomorrow morning. Reid's filing a report right now, or else he'd speak with you himself."

Polly knew better. "Tell him congratulations. You too, Fran. Does Tom know?"

"I called him first. I can't wait to see him. We're going to watch the news in bed tomorrow morning."

After she had hung up, Polly sat on the bed, her head in her hands. "Thank you, Lord."

Reid was fine. The last chapter was closed. She could go on with her life. Too drained to drive, she lay down on the bed to wait for morning. After she watched the news, she was going home. Back to her nice, orderly life. Without Reid.

She lay on the bed, Cuddles curled up at her side. She was crying softly. Cuddles was snoring loudly.

Some time in the middle of the night Cuddles started making a racket. His barking awoke Polly. The room was pitch-dark, only a slant of light coming through the slit where the drapes failed to close. In her sleep-fogged state, she thought he was barking awfully loud. Then she realized the racket wasn't coming from Cuddles alone. Someone was banging on the door.

She sat up fast. She groped for the phone to call the police, but knocked it onto the floor instead. Who would be banging on the door at this hour? Disoriented, she switched on the lamp near the bed and leaned down to grab the phone.

"Open up, Polly," a male voice shouted from the other side of the door. "It's me. Open the freakin' door before I bang it down."

Holding the receiver, her hand froze in midair. She'd know that silky, imperious, autocratic cop voice anywhere. Her heart skipped into overdrive.

"Why should I?" she shouted, dropping the phone on the nightstand.

"Because."

"Because is no answer." She raced into the bathroom and splashed water on her face.

"You want the whole world to hear me, fine! I've had a long time to think over our future."

Our future. "You call two days a long time?" Frantic, she dived for her purse. She dumped the contents onto the bed. Shoving aside her lipstick, comb, food coupons, wallet, credit-card holder, penlight, pad, pencil, address book, she found her perfume atomizer. Arching her neck, she gave herself a spritz.

"You're damned right," he answered. "Stop this nonsense. I'm in love with you."

Her heart stopped. When it restarted, she flew to the door and flung it open. Reid stood there, grinning sexily, one arm propped high, the other twirling a rose.

She yanked him inside the room and shut the door. "What did you say?"

He crushed her in his arms and began kissing her before she could say another word. When he released her, he rubbed his cheek against hers. "I couldn't lose you."

He felt wonderful, warm and vibrantly alive. "Not that part. What did you say before then?"

"I understand you know the story of how my father didn't propose to my mother."

"Reid, go back to the beginning."

"My pleasure." He gave her a soul-deep kiss that curled her toes.

When her eyes opened, he was smiling at her. "Before then," she murmured, her hands racing over him, making sure he was truly all right.

"Oh, you mean the part where I said I love you."

She grabbed his face between her hands. Her eyes devoured him. "That's the part. Say it again."

He kissed her, murmuring over and over that he loved her. "Sweetheart, I know times have changed. I respect feminism, but you'd better know right now, this isn't a proposal."

Her head reared back. "I will not—"

"You will. Calm down, tiger. We're getting married."

She opened her mouth. He kissed it shut, sending shock waves of desire pouring through her.

"No, there's no room for discussion," he said, repeating the words she had used with him. "While I waited for Grayson and those goons to show, all I could think about was catching them so I could be with you."

"Fran told me about the Guns N' Roses tape."

"I didn't think Horace would mind. This was my last case. I'm putting in my resignation papers from the state police. I hear the Prosecutor's Office in town is looking for a good attorney. I'm applying. I'm also contacting Judge Joyce. He loves cops. He'll especially look kindly on one who helped catch Grayson and his bosses red-handed. We have an airtight case."

She wouldn't think of interrupting him. He was handing her her dream.

"I know," he went on, "that you've got this crazy notion that people need to know everything about each other first, but you're wrong. In fifty years we'll still be discovering things about each other. You're exciting. You're wonderful, and you're mine."

"Yours?" she repeated, loving the way his hot gaze roamed over her body.

"I can't help the way I think. I'm selfish. We found something rare and beautiful. Why let it go? Tell me before I go crazy. Do you think you can learn to love me?"

Her arms held him tight. Her lips trembled with mirth. "No."

His eyes narrowed. "No?"

"No."

He shook her. "You're serious?"

"Mmmm, yes. Very. I'm afraid you're too late," she said merrily.

He groaned. "Don't tease me. I can't take it. I was more afraid driving here than I was capturing the crooks."

She stroked his face and gazed at him in adoration, thinking her life was as thrilling as the heroine's in her romance book.

"I already love you, Reid. I've loved you since before we made love. It broke my heart to leave you."

His mouth came down on hers in celebration. "Martha's going to get her wish," he said, his voice husky.

She snuggled in his arms. "Is she, darling?"

He picked up her hand, linking their pinkie fingers. His eyes shone with love. "Mmmm. Shall I prove it?"

"I thought you'd never ask. . . ."

THE EDITOR'S CORNER

The bounty of six LOVESWEPTs coming your way next month is sure to put you in the right mood for the holiday season. Emotional and exciting, sensuous and scintillating, these tales of love and romance guarantee hours of unbeatable reading pleasure. So indulge yourself—there's no better way to start the celebration!

Leading our lineup is Charlotte Hughes with **KISSED BY A ROGUE**, LOVESWEPT #654—and a rogue is exactly what Cord Buford is. With a smile that promises wicked pleasures, he's used to getting what he wants, so when the beautiful new physician in town insists she won't go out with him, he takes it as a very personal challenge. He'll do anything to feel Billie Foster's soft hands on him, even dare her to give him a physical. Billie's struggle to resist Cord's dangerous temptations is useless, but when their investigation into a mystery at his family's textile mill erupts into steamy kisses under moonlit skies, she has to wonder if she's the one woman who can tame his wild heart. Charlotte's talent shines brightly in this delicious romance.

New author Debra Dixon makes an outstanding debut in LOVESWEPT with **TALL, DARK, AND LONESOME**, #655. Trail boss Zach Weston is definitely all of those things, as Niki Devlin soon discovers when she joins his vacation cattle drive. The columnist starts out interested only in getting a story, but from the moment Zach pulls her out of the mud and into his arms, she wants to scorch his iron control and play with the fire in his gray eyes. However, she believes the scandal that haunts her past can destroy his dreams of happily-ever-after—until Zach dares her to stop running and be lassoed by his love. Talented Debra combines emotional intensity and humor to make **TALL, DARK, AND LONESOME** a winner. You're sure to look forward to more from this New Face of 1993!

Do you remember Jenny Love-Townsend, the heroine's daughter in Peggy Webb's **TOUCHED BY ANGELS**? She returns in **A PRINCE FOR JENNY**, LOVESWEPT #656, but now she's all grown up, a fragile artist who finally meets the man of her dreams. Daniel Sullivan is everything she's ever wished for and the one thing she's sure she can't have. Daniel agrees that the spellbinding emotion between them can't last. He doesn't consider himself to be as noble, strong, and powerful as Jenny sketched him, and though he wants to taste her magic, his desire for this special woman can put her in danger. Peggy will have you crying and cheering as these two people find the courage to believe in the power of love.

What an apt title **FEVER** is for Joan J. Domning's new LOVESWEPT #657, for the temperature does nothing but rise when Alec Golightly and Bunny Fletcher meet. He's a corporate executive who wears a Hawaiian shirt and a pirate's grin—not at all what she expects when she goes to Portland to help bail out his company. Her plan is to get the job done, then quickly return to the fast track, but she suddenly finds herself wildly tempted to run into his arms and stay there. A family is one thing she's never had time for in her race to be the best, but with Alec tantalizing her with his long, slow kisses, she's ready to seize the happiness that has always eluded her. Joan delivers a sexy romance that burns white-hot with desire.

Please welcome Jackie Reeser and her very first novel, **THE LADY CASTS HER LURES**, LOVESWEPT #658. Jackie's a veteran journalist, and she has given her heroine, Pat Langston, the same occupation—and a vexing assignment: to accompany champion Brian Culler on the final round of a fishing contest. He's always found reporters annoying, but one look at Pat and he quickly welcomes the delectable distraction, baiting her with charm that could reel any woman in. The spirited single mom isn't interested in a lady's man who'd never settle down, though. But Brian knows all about being patient and pursues her with seductive humor, willing to wait for the prize of her passion. This delightful romance, told with plenty of verve and sensuality, will show you why we're so excited to be publishing Jackie in LOVESWEPT.

Diane Pershing rounds out the lineup in a very big way with **HEARTQUAKE**, LOVESWEPT #659. A golden-haired geologist, David Franklin prowls the earth in search of the secrets that make it tremble, but he's never felt a tremor as strong as the one that shakes his very soul when he meets Bella Stein. A distant relative, she's surprised by his arrival on her doorstep—and shocked by the restless longing he awakens in her. His wildfire caresses make the beautiful widow respond to him with shameless abandon. Then she discovers the pain he's hidden from everyone, and only her tenderness can heal him and show him that he's worthy of her gift of enduring love. . . . Diane's evocative writing makes this romance stand out.

Happy reading,

With warmest wishes,

Nita Taublib

Nita Taublib

Associate Publisher

P.S. Don't miss the spectacular women's novels Bantam has coming in December: **ADAM'S FALL** by Sandra Brown, a classic romance soon to be available in hardcover; **NOTORIOUS** by Patricia Potter, in which the rivalry and passion between two saloon owners becomes the rage of San Francisco; **PRINCESS OF THIEVES** by Katherine O'Neal, featuring a delightfully wicked con woman and a rugged, ruthless bounty hunter; and **CAPTURE THE NIGHT** by Geralyn Dawson, the latest Once Upon a Time romance with "Beauty and the Beast" at its heart. We'll be giving you a sneak peak at these terrific books in next month's LOVESWEPTs. And immediately following this page, look for a preview of the exciting women's fiction from Bantam *available now!*

"Susan Johnson brings sensuality to new heights and beyond."
—*Romantic Times*

Susan Johnson

Nationally bestselling author of
SINFUL and **SILVER FLAME**

Outlaw

Susan Johnson's most passionate and richly textured romance yet, OUTLAW is the sizzling story of a fierce Scottish border lord who abducts his sworn enemy, a beautiful English woman—only to find himself a captive of her love.

"Come sit by me then." Elizabeth gently patted the rough bark beside her as if coaxing a small child to an unpleasant task.

He should leave, Johnnie thought. He shouldn't have ridden after her, he shouldn't be panting like a dog in heat for any woman . . . particularly for this woman, the daughter of Harold Godfrey, his lifelong enemy.

"Are you afraid of me?" She'd stopped running now from her desire. It was an enormous leap of faith, a rash and venturesome sensation for a woman who'd always viewed the world with caution.

"I'm not afraid of anything," Johnnie answered, unhesitating confidence in his deep voice.

"I didn't think so," she replied. Dressed like a reiver in leather breeches, high boots, a shirt open at the throat, his hunting plaid the muted color of autumn foliage, he looked not only unafraid but menacing. The danger and attraction of scandalous sin, she thought—all dark arrogant masculinity. "My guardsmen will wait indefinitely," she said very, very quietly, thinking with an arrogance of her own, There. That should move him.

And when he took that first step, she smiled a tantalizing female smile, artless and instinctive.

"You please me," she said, gazing up at him as he slowly drew near.

"*You* drive me mad," Johnnie said, sitting down on the fallen tree, resting his arms on his knees and contemplating the dusty toes of his boots.

"And you don't like the feeling."

"I dislike it intensely," he retorted, chafing resentment plain in his voice.

He wouldn't look at her. "Would you rather I leave?"

His head swiveled toward her then, a cynical gleam in his blue eyes. "Of course not."

"Hmmm," Elizabeth murmured, pursing her lips, clasping her hands together and studying her yellow kidskin slippers. "This *is* awkward," she said after a moment, amusement in her voice. Sitting up straighter, she half turned to gaze at him. "I've never seduced a man before." A smile of unalloyed innocence curved her mouth. "Could you help me? If you don't mind, my lord," she demurely added.

A grin slowly creased his tanned cheek. "You play the ingenue well, Lady Graham," he said, sitting upright to better meet her frankly sensual gaze. His pale blue eyes had warmed, restoring a goodly measure of his charm. "I'd be a damned fool to mind," he said, his grin in sharp contrast to the curious affection in his eyes.

Exhaling theatrically, Elizabeth said, "Thank you, my lord," in a blatant parody of gratitude. "Without your assistance I despaired of properly arousing you."

He laughed, a warm-hearted sound of natural pleasure. "On that count you needn't have worried. I've been in rut since I left Edinburgh to see you."

"Could I be of some help?" she murmured, her voice husky, enticing.

He found himself attentively searching the ground for a suitable place to lie with her. "I warn you," he said very low, his mouth in a lazy grin, "I'm days past the need for seduction. All I can offer you is this country setting. Do you mind?"

She smiled up at him as she put her hand in his. "As long as you hold me, my lord, and as long as the grass stains don't show."

He paused for a moment with her small hand light on his palm. "You're very remarkable," he softly said.

"Too candid for you, my lord?" she playfully inquired.

His long fingers closed around her hand in an act of possession, pure and simple, as if he would keep this spirited, plain-speaking woman who startled him. "Your candor excites me," he said. "Be warned," he murmured, drawing her to her feet. "I've been wanting you for three days' past; I won't guarantee finesse." Releasing her hand, he held his up so she could see them tremble. "Look."

"I'm shaking *inside* so violently I may savage you first, my lord," Elizabeth softly breathed, swaying toward him, her fragrance sweet in his nostrils, her face lifted for a kiss. "I've been waiting four months since I left Goldiehouse."

A spiking surge of lust ripped through his senses, gut-deep, searing, her celibacy a singular, flamboyant ornament offered to him as if it were his duty, his obligation to bring her pleasure. In a flashing moment his hands closed on her shoulders. Pulling her sharply close, his palms slid down her back— then lower, swiftly cupping her bottom. His mouth dipped to hers and he forced her mouth open, plunging his tongue deep inside.

Like a woman too long denied, Elizabeth welcomed him, pulling his head down so she could reach his mouth more easily, straining upward on tiptoes so she could feel him hard against her, tearing at the buttons on his shirt so the heat of his skin touched hers.

"Hurry, Johnnie, please . . ." she whispered.

Moonlight, Madness, & Magic
by
Suzanne Foster, Charlotte Hughes, and Olivia Rupprecht

"A beguiling mix of passion and the occult. . . . an engaging read."
—*Publishers Weekly*
"Incredibly ingenious." —*Romantic Times*

This strikingly original anthology by three of Loveswept's bestselling authors is one of the most talked about books of the year! With more than 2.5 million copies of their titles in print, these beloved authors bring their talents to a boldly imaginative collection of romantic novellas that weaves a tale of witchcraft, passion, and unconditional love set in 1785, 1872, and 1992.

Here's a look at the heart-stopping prologue . . . .

OXFORD VILLAGE, MASSACHUSETTS — 1690 Rachael Deliverance Dobbs had been beautiful once. The flaming red hair that often strayed from her morning cap and curled in wispy tendrils about her face had turned more than one shop-keeper's head. Today, however, that red hair was tangled and filthy and fell against her back and shoulders like a tattered woolen shawl.

Prison had not served her well.

"The woman hath *witchcraft* in her," an onlooker spat out as Rachael was led to the front of the meeting house, where a constable, the governor's magistrate, and several of the town selectmen waited to decide her fate. Her ankles were shackled in irons, making her progress slow and painful.

Rachael staggered, struggling to catch her balance as the magistrate peered over his spectacles at her. Clearing his throat, the magistrate began to speak, giving each word a deep and thunderous import. "Rachael Deliverance Dobbs, thou hast been accused by this court of not fearing the Almighty God as do thy good and prudent neighbors, of preternatural acts against the citizenry of Oxford, and of the heinous crime of witchcraft, for which, by the law of the colony of Massachusetts, thou deservest to die. Has thou anything to say in thy defense?"

Rachael Dobbs could barely summon the strength to deny the charges. Her accusers had kept her jailed for months, often depriving her of sleep, food, and clean water to drink. In order to secure a confession, they'd whipped her with rawhide and tortured her with hideous instruments. Though she'd been grievously injured and several of her ribs broken, she'd given them nothing.

"Nay," she said faintly, "I know not of which ye speak, m'lord. For as God is my witness, I have been wrongly accused."

A rage quickened the air, and several of the spectators rose from their seats. "Blasphemy!" someone cried. "The witch would use *His* name in vain?"

"Order!" The magistrate brought his gavel down. "Let the accused answer the charges. Goody Dobbs, it is said thou makest the devil's brew of strange plants that grow in the forest."

"I know not this devil's brew you speak of," Rachael protested. "I use the herbs for healing, just as my mother before me."

"And thou extracts a fungus from rye grass to stop birthing pains?" he queried.

"I do not believe a woman should suffer so, m'lord."

"Even though the Good Book commands it?"

"The Good Book also commands us to use the sense God gave us," she reminded him tremulously.

"I'll not tolerate this sacrilege!" The village preacher slammed his fist down on the table, inciting the onlookers into a frenzy of shouting and name-calling.

As the magistrate called for order, Rachael turned to the crowd, searching for the darkly handsome face of her betrothed, Jonathan Nightingale. She'd not been allowed visitors in jail, but surely Jonathan would be here today to speak on her behalf. With his wealth and good name, he would quickly put an end to this hysteria. That hope had kept her alive, bringing her comfort even when she'd learned her children had been placed in the care of Jonathan's housekeeper, a young woman Rachael distrusted for her deceptive ways. But that mattered little now. When Jonathaan cleared her name of these crimes, she would be united with her babes once again. How she longed to see them!

"Speak thou for me, Jonathan Nightingale?" she cried, forgetting everything but her joy at seeing him. "Thou knowest me better than anyone. Thou knowest the secrets of my heart. Tell these people I am not what they accuse me. Tell them, so that my children may be returned to me." Her voice trembled with emotion, but as Jonathan glanced up and met her eyes, she knew a moment of doubt. She didn't see the welcoming warmth she expected. Was something amiss?

At the magistrate's instruction, the bailiff called Jonathan to come forward. "State thy name for the court," the bailiff said, once he'd been sworn in.

"Jonathan Peyton Nightingale."

"Thou knowest the accused, Goody Dobbs?" the magistrate asked.

Jonathan acknowledged Rachael with a slow nod of his head. "Mistress Dobbs and I were engaged to be married before she was incarcerated," Jonathan told the magistrate. "I've assumed the care of her children these last few months. She has no family of her own."

"Hast thou anything to say in her defense?"

"She was a decent mother, to be sure. Her children be well mannered."

"And have ye reason to believe the charges against her?"

When Jonathan hesitated, the magistrate pressed him. "Prithee, do not withhold information from the court, Mr. Nightingale," he cautioned, "lest thee find thyself in the same dire predicament as the accused. Conspiring to protect a witch is a lawful test of guilt."

Startled, Jonathan could only stare at the stern-faced tribunal before him. It had never occured to him that his association with Rachael could put him in a hangman's noose as well. He had been searching his soul since she'd been jailed, wondering how much he was morally bound to reveal at this trial. Now he saw little choice but to unburden himself.

"After she was taken, I found this among her things," he said, pulling an object from his coat pocket and unwrapping it. He avoided looking at Rachael, anticipating the stricken expression he would surely see in her eyes. "It's an image made of horsehair. A woman's image. There be a pin stuck through it."

The crowd gasped as Jonathan held up the effigy. A woman screamed, and even the magistrate drew back in horror.

Rachael sat in stunned disbelief. An icy fist closed around her heart. How could Jonathan have done such a thing? Did he not realize he'd signed her death warrant? Dear merciful God, if they found her guilty, she would never see her children again!

" 'Twas mere folly that I fashioned the image, m'lord," she told the magistrate. "I suspected my betrothed of dallying with his housekeeper. I fear my temper bested me."

"And was it folly when thou gavest Goodwife Brown's child the evil eye and caused her to languish with the fever?" the magistrate probed.

" 'Twas coincidence, m'lord," she said, imploring him to believe her. "The child was ill when I arrived at Goody Brown's house. I merely tried to help her." Rachael could see the magistrate's skepticism, and she whirled to Jonathan in desperation. "How canst thou doubt me, Jonathan?" she asked.

He hung his head. He was torn with regret, even shame. He loved Rachael, but God help him, he had no wish to die beside her. One had only to utter the word *witch* these days to end up on the gallows. Not that Rachael hadn't given all of them cause to suspect her. When he'd found the effigy, he'd told himself she must have been maddened by jealousy. But truly he didn't understand her anymore. She'd stopped going to Sunday services and more than once had induced him to lie abed with her on a Sabbath morn. "Methinks thou hast bewitched me as well, Rachael," he replied.

Another gasp from the crowd.

"Hanging is too good for her!" a woman shouted.

"Burn her!" another cried from the front row. "Before she bewitches us all."

Rachael bent her head in despair, all hope draining from her. Her own betrothed had forsaken her, and his condemnation meant certain death. There was no one who could save her now. And yet, in the depths of her desolation, a spark of rage kindled.

"So be it," she said, seized by a black hysteria. She was beyond caring now, beyond the crowd's censure or their grace. No one could take anything more from her than had already been taken. Jonathan's engagement gift to her, a golden locket, hung at her neck. She ripped it free and flung it at him.

"Thou shall have thy desire, Jonathan Nightingale," she cried. "And pay for it dearly. Since thou hast consigned me to the gallows and stolen my children from me, I shall put a blood curse on thee and thine."

The magistrate pounded his gavel against the table, ordering the spectators to silence. "Mistress Dobbs!" he warned, his voice harsh, "I fear thou hast just sealed thy fate."

But Rachael would not be deterred. Her heart was aflame with the fury of a woman betrayed. "Hear me good, Jonathan," she said, oblivious of the magistrate, of everyone but the man she'd once loved with all her being. "Thou hast damned my soul to hell, but I'll not burn there alone. I curse the Nightingale seed to a fate worse than the flames of Hades. Your progeny shall be as the living dead, denied the rest of the grave."

Her voice dropped to a terrifying hush as she began to intone the curse. "The third son of every third son shall walk the earth as a creature of the night, trapped in shadows, no two creatures alike. Stripped of humanity, he will howl in concert with demons, never to die, always to wander in agony, until a woman entraps his heart and soul as thee did mine—"

"My God, she is truly the devil's mistress!" the preacher gasped. A cry rose from the crowd, and several of them surged forward, trying to stop her. Guards rushed to block them.

"Listen to me, Jonathan!" Rachael cried over the din. "I've not finished with thee yet. If that woman should find a way to set the creature free, it will be at great and terrible cost. A sacrifice no mortal woman would ever be willing to make—"

She hesitated, her chin beginning to tremble as hot tears pooled in her eyes. Glistening, they slid down her cheeks, burning her tender flesh before they dropped to the wooden floor. But as they hit the planks, something astonishing happened. Even

Rachael in her grief was amazed. The teardrops hardened before everyone's eyes into precious gems. Flashing in the sunlight was a dazzling blue-white diamond, a blood-red ruby, and a brilliant green emerald.

The crowd was stunned to silence.

Rachael glanced up, aware of Jonathan's fear, of everyone's astonishment. Their gaping stares brought her a fleeting sense of triumph. Her curse had been heard.

"Rachael Dobbs, confess thy sins before this court and thy Creator!" the magistrate bellowed.

But it was too late for confessions. The doors to the courtroom burst open, and a pack of men streamed in with blazing pine torches. "Goody Brown's child is dead of the fits," they shouted. "The witch must burn!"

The guards couldn't hold back the vigilantes, and Rachael closed her eyes as the pack of men engulfed her. She said a silent good-bye to her children as she was gripped by bruising hands and lifted off the ground. She could feel herself being torn nearly apart as they dragged her from the meeting room, but she did not cry out. She felt no physical pain. She had just made a pact with the forces of darkness, and she could no longer feel anything except the white-hot inferno of the funeral pyre that would soon release her to her everlasting vigil.

She welcomed it, just as she welcomed the sweet justice that would one day be hers. She would not die in vain. Her curse had been heard.

"Fayrene Preston has an uncanny ability
to create intense atmosphere that
is truly superb."
—*Romantic Times*

Satin and Steele
by
Fayrene Preston

SATIN AND STEELE *is a classic favorite of fans of
Fayrene Preston. Originally published under the pseud-
onym Jaelyn Conlee, this novel was the talented Ms.
Preston's first ever published novel. We are thrilled to
offer you the opportunity to read this long-unavailable
book in its new Bantam edition.*

Skye Anderson knew the joy and wonder of love—as
well as the pain of its tragic loss. She'd carved a new
life for herself at Dallas' Hayes Corporation, finding
security in a cocoon of hard-working days and lonely
nights. Then her company is taken over by the leg-
endary corporate raider James Steele and once again
Skye must face the possibility of losing everything
she cares about. When Steele enlists her aid in
organizing the new company, she is determined to
prove herself worthy of the challenge. But as they
work together side by side, Skye can't deny that
she feels more than a professional interest in her

new boss—and that the feeling is mutual. Soon she would have to decide whether to let go of her desire for Steele once and for all—or risk everything for a second chance at love.

And don't miss these heart-stopping
romances from Bantam Books,
on sale in November:

ADAM'S FALL
a new hardcover edition of the Sandra
Brown classic!

NOTORIOUS
by Patricia Potter
The *Romantic Times* 1992
"Storyteller of the Year"

PRINCESS OF THIEVES
by Katherine O'Neal
"A brilliant new talent bound to make her
mark on the genre." —Iris Johansen

CAPTURE THE NIGHT
by Geralyn Dawson
"A fresh and delightful new author!
GOLD 5 stars"
—*Heartland Critiques*

and in hardcover from Doubleday

ON WINGS OF MAGIC
a classic romance by Kay Hooper

OFFICIAL RULES

To enter the sweepstakes below carefully follow all instructions found elsewhere in this offer.

The **Winners Classic** will award prizes with the following approximate maximum values: 1 Grand Prize: $26,500 (or $25,000 cash alternate); 1 First Prize: $3,000; 5 Second Prizes: $400 each; 35 Third Prizes: $100 each; 1,000 Fourth Prizes: $7.50 each. Total maximum retail value of Winners Classic Sweepstakes is $42,500. Some presentations of this sweepstakes may contain individual entry numbers corresponding to one or more of the aforementioned prize levels. To determine the Winners, individual entry numbers will first be compared with the winning numbers preselected by computer. For winning numbers not returned, prizes will be awarded in random drawings from among all eligible entries received. Prize choices may be offered at various levels. If a winner chooses an automobile prize, all license and registration fees, taxes, destination charges and, other expenses not offered herein are the responsibility of the winner. If a winner chooses a trip, travel must be complete within one year from the time the prize is awarded. Minors must be accompanied by an adult. Travel companion(s) must also sign release of liability. Trips are subject to space and departure availability. Certain black-out dates may apply.

The following applies to the sweepstakes named above:

No purchase necessary. You can also enter the sweepstakes by sending your name and address to: P.O. Box 508, Gibbstown, N.J. 08027. Mail each entry separately. Sweepstakes begins 6/1/93. Entries must be received by 12/30/94. Not responsible for lost, late, damaged, misdirected, illegible or postage due mail. Mechanically reproduced entries are not eligible. All entries become property of the sponsor and will not be returned.

Prize Selection/Validations: Selection of winners will be conducted no later than 5:00 PM on January 28, 1995, by an independent judging organization whose decisions are final. Random drawings will be held at 1211 Avenue of the Americas, New York, N.Y. 10036. Entrants need not be present to win. Odds of winning are determined by total number of entries received. Circulation of this sweepstakes is estimated not to exceed 200 million. All prizes are guaranteed to be awarded and delivered to winners. Winners will be notified by mail and may be required to complete an affidavit of eligibility and release of liability which must be returned within 14 days of date on notification or alternate winners will be selected in a random drawing. Any prize notification letter or any prize returned to a participating sponsor, Bantam Doubleday Dell Publishing Group, Inc., its participating divisions or subsidiaries, or the independent judging organization as undeliverable will be awarded to an alternate winner. Prizes are not transferable. No substitution for prizes except as offered or as may be necessary due to unavailability, in which case a prize of equal or greater value will be awarded. Prizes will be awarded approximately 90 days after the drawing. All taxes are the sole responsibility of the winners. Entry constitutes permission (except where prohibited by law) to use winners' names, hometowns, and likenesses for publicity purposes without further or other compensation. Prizes won by minors will be awarded in the name of parent or legal guardian.

Participation: Sweepstakes open to residents of the United States and Canada, except for the province of Quebec. Sweepstakes sponsored by Bantam Doubleday Dell Publishing Group, Inc., (BDD), 1540 Broadway, New York, NY 10036. Versions of this sweepstakes with different graphics and prize choices will be offered in conjunction with various solicitations or promotions by different subsidiaries and divisions of BDD. Where applicable, winners will have their choice of any prize offered at level won. Employees of BDD, its divisions, subsidiaries, advertising agencies, independent judging organization, and their immediate family members are not eligible.

Canadian residents, in order to win, must first correctly answer a time limited arithmetical skill testing question. Void in Puerto Rico, Quebec and wherever prohibited or restricted by law. Subject to all federal, state, local and provincial laws and regulations. For a list of major prize winners (available after 1/29/95): send a self-addressed, stamped envelope entirely separate from your entry to: Sweepstakes Winners, P.O. Box 517, Gibbstown, NJ 08027. Requests must be received by 12/30/94. DO NOT SEND ANY OTHER CORRESPONDENCE TO THIS P.O. BOX.

SWP 7/93

Don't miss these fabulous Bantam women's fiction titles

on sale in November

• NOTORIOUS

by Patricia Potter, author of *RENEGADE*

Long ago, Catalina Hilliard had vowed never to give away her heart, but she hadn't counted on the spark of desire that flared between her and her business rival, Marsh Canton. Now that desire is about to spin Cat's carefully orchestrated life out of control.

_____ 56225-8 $5.50/6.50 in Canada

• PRINCESS OF THIEVES

by Katherine O'Neal, author of *THE LAST HIGHWAYMAN*

Mace Blackwood was a daring rogue—the greatest con artist in the world. Saranda Sherwin was a master thief who used her wits and wiles to make tough men weak. And when Saranda's latest charade leads to tragedy and sends her fleeing for her life, Mace is compelled to follow, no matter what the cost.

_____ 56066-2 $5.50/$6.50 in Canada

• CAPTURE THE NIGHT

by Geralyn Dawson

In this "Once Upon a Time" Romance with "Beauty and the Beast" at its heart, Geralyn Dawson weaves the love story of a runaway beauty, the Texan who rescues her, and their precious stolen "Rose."

_____ 56176-6 $4.99/5.99 in Canada

Ask for these books at your local bookstore or use this page to order.

❑ Please send me the books I have checked above. I am enclosing $ _____ (add $2.50 to cover postage and handling). Send check or money order, no cash or C. O. D.'s please.

Name _____

Address _____

City/ State/ Zip _____

Send order to: Bantam Books, Dept. FN121, 2451 S. Wolf Rd., Des Plaines, IL 60018
Allow four to six weeks for delivery.
Prices and availability subject to change without notice.

DORIS PARMETT

I was brought up in a family of readers and writers. It was the most natural thing in the world for me to seek out a good book to enjoy on a daily basis.

Over the years I've written a series of children's books, poems, and magazine articles. I enjoy reading all genres, particularly the romance genre. I'm especially interested in bringing people together in their quest for love and understanding. Let's face it, I have a husband who brags that he provides much of my material.

The day my husband and I met he announced he intended to marry me. I laughed. He didn't. Seven months after his announcement we were married. Two children, and I refuse to say how many years later, we're still married.

After I graduated from college in New Jersey, we headed west to live in California. From there we headed to Texas, and in time we returned to California, where I received a master's degree from the University of Southern California and began my teaching career. Eventually we found ourselves back east where it all started.

Combining the varied roles of wife, mother, teacher, and now writer, has not always been easy, but it's never been boring!

So here I am, off and running, a new ribbon in my printer and my word processor poised at the ready: "Once upon a time..."

REID—A Heartbreaker Cop Who Kissed Like the Hero of a Hot Romance...

He'd only intended to silence Polly Sweet's sassy mouth with a pretend smooch, but undercover state trooper Reid Cameron's scheme backfired! He'd invaded her privacy—and her fantasies—when he'd commandeered her house to catch a jewel thief, but when he decided they'd play lovers and tried to teach the feisty spitfire a lesson about feigning passion, both were shocked by the fireworks their lips set off!

A Lawman Who Left Her Breathless

Insisting she was only doing research for the stories she wrote, that she preferred polite, poetic blonds to tall, dark, and dangerous, Polly denied that anything was happening between them, no matter how good Reid looked in jeans! He made her sizzle with desire and kissed like a dream, but could the bravest man she'd ever met persuade the lady who'd stolen his heart that he'd found heaven in her arms?

Loveswept

*Love stories you'll never forget,
by authors you'll always remember.*

ISBN 0-553-44251-1

44251

0 76783 00350 7